CHECKMATE

L. R. STARR

 Created with Vellum

I want to dedicate this book to all the fast-paced plot lovers out there. All the lovers of the written word. All those who read books cover to cover. To all those who turn the pages greedily waiting for the next installment. Those who love a good dose of wit, action, and suspense. I warn you this is a cliff hanger, so prepare yourself for the next one.

1

SARA

L et me tell you a little story about when I fell for a bad guy...Yeah, I know right? Pretty cliché, good girl falls for bad guy. Stay with me, because it's a *helluva* story and not what you think. Honestly.

I met Evana Herold in a cool, hip downtown bar in New York. The vibe was chilled, the beautiful people were there. You know the type: guys with tailored custom-made suits, polka dot kerchiefs, and black patent loafers. No socks. Side parts slicked back behind their ears. Fresh baby-faced play-boys, cocky, full of testosterone, looking to score with a beau-tiful insecure model with a gap in her teeth. Money was no object and hopefully, her friends didn't mind a *ménage a trois*. I rolled my eyes at the thought. I felt like I was in a photo-shoot. Sweet melancholic tunes of Lana Del Ray permeated the bar. The irony of the song choice wasn't lost on me; I smiled wryly as the song 'Young and Beautiful' caressed my eardrums.

When I walked in, my simple black dress, work cleavage, and pearl earrings took a backseat to the glamor pusses in the room. My shoulder-length mahogany brown hair sat up in a ponytail with a clip holding it together strategically. Nothing too fancy. Out of my face, the way I liked it. Black pumps, usually quite effective I might add – although it didn't feel enough that night. I jostled through the Young and Restless cast with cosmos in their hands, scanning the crowd. Evana sat at a table towards the back of the bar. I took in her ruby red nails and elegant slender fingers wrapped around a cigarette. She stared through the crowd with a detached look, not seeming to mind that ash fell on her silver sequin dress. She bit her bottom lip as if she is going to chew straight through it. This couldn't be the confident *Vogue* model that everyone kept raving about, could it?

Her face was pale, almost ghostlike, but at the same time strangely ethereal. Silver glitter was creased into her eyelids, complimenting her futuristic look. She looked like she didn't eat much. I imagined the nervous energy she held inside was enough to keep her weight in check. Her medium-length blond hair lay crimped and swept away from her angular face; her luminous azure eyes locked with mine as I approached. She gave me a painful tight smile as the recognition from the photos set in.

"Hi. Evana, right?"

"Maurice thought it would be nice for us to meet."

She regarded me coolly: a slow eye scan, top to toe as she took a dramatic drag on her cigarette and blew it up and out to the left.

"Did he now?" Suspicion arose on Evans angular face, while her eyes remained distant.

Complicated and delicate was the premise of this new case, with a stuck-up model to boot.

Before I get started, let's circle back. To Evana, I was the new *Vogue* intern and personal assistant, sent to keep her in check and make sure she arrived on time for shoots. A babysitter to the stars. *Go me.*

Evana reluctantly summoned me to meet her at the bar. Maurice sent photos across, which is how she recognized me. Strange that she came alone. I pictured her having a pack of salivating hungry male wolves hunting her, and a bevy of attractive women as her bosom buddies.

Maurice, the Creative Director at Vogue agreed to support the cover in cooperation with my client. He had known Maurice for many years, and they had a long friendship. His involvement in the case was severely limited, however.

"Just get her in the door and let her do her job." That's all Maurice knew.

I'm sorry, we haven't formally been introduced. I'm Sara; no-nonsense, socially awkward, badass private investigator. I sometimes take on high profile cases that haven't received justice in the courtroom. I work entirely too hard, love coffee and a muffin or two. I have a 98% track record in case resolution with no life to boot. The 2% I don't wanna get into right now. I'm the one you want when the law has been exhausted. Nice to meet you. Current case suspect and primary lead: Evana's husband. Enter stage left: *Robert Elliot*.

My client lost his case for the murder of his son, Michael Sawyer. He was a tech nerd who worked for Mescon Technologies. A nine-to-five type eat-your-homemade-lunch-in-a-brown-paper-bag man. Blink and you would miss him. But we all have our secrets. Michael's must have been mighty juicy if he was in cahoots with Robert Elliot. He was killed gruesomely, legs and arms chopped off – that type of thing. Yep, like a movie scene reenacted out of Saw. Baggies of body parts found floating in the Hudson river by an over-eager solo swimmer on a Sunday morning. Who swims in the Hudson anyway? Everybody knows it's a cesspool of trash! Why hadn't the case gone to the cops you ask? *Complications*. My client didn't trust the cops – he sensed they were in on it. He wanted me to track Elliot as he suspected the murder to be his handiwork. He had a long history with the Elliot's. That's where I swung into the picture.

Now back to the bar...

Evana's look of disdain indicated she wasn't keen on my outfit. I had to work at gaining her trust. She was super-hot right now in the model game. She was on the cover of everything. *And I mean evvvvver-ree-thing.* Vogue Paris, Vogue Milan, Vogue New York and Rolling Stone.

"So, this bar is something huh?" I mentally slapped my forehead. I needed to go through my Rolodex of verbal etiquette for supermodels. Not my greatest opening line.

"Look, I want to be clear. I really don't need some shabby little assistant following me around like a puppy dog. Just stay outta my way and we won't have any problems." She waved her ruby reds towards the sky like she was flicking away a mosquito.

I don't care what you want brat. I'm here to serve the client and investigate your potential scumbag of a husband. Mental telepathy probably wasn't one of Evana's strong suits. I felt safe.

I tried again. "So. What do models do for fun, Evana?" *What was I saying? I had interviewed enough clients and suspects to know better than this!* Evana gave me a petulant look that said it all.

"Coke." I almost spat out my drink. Easier than I thought. I mean models and coke is fitting the stereotype so far, right?

Evana smirked. "Urghhh, come on, don't tell me you're *that* green."

I upped the ante. "No, I'm a casual user." *Never tried the stuff in my life.* I didn't plan on it either, but for the purpose of the case, I had to act the part. I leaned forward and pretended to be wide-eyed, looking up to her. I whispered.

"Know where I can get a little stash to add to my supply?"

"Come by my house tomorrow night if you want," she replied nonchalantly. "I will introduce you to some of my crew. You can meet my husband," she softened slightly in tone.

Crazy how after ten minutes of talking, this model, not knowing me from a pair of Victoria's Secret underwear, wanted me to join her for a drug party. *BINGO*. Step one of my covert operation started smoothly.

"Ok," I piped up. "I wouldn't miss it for the world. I'll be there with bells on." As you can probably tell, I'm a little awkward in social situations. *Bells on?* Time to employ a different approach. Evana skimmed over me with a disinterested look. Seemed like an exit plan was in action. She moved her eyes past me, looking straight at the bathroom. Probably ready to re-jolt her system. A few moments later, a leggy model approached and Evana's face lit up like a Christmas tree.

"Soooo, I gotta run now, be at my house by eight tomorrow night, Maurice will give you the address." She glanced back smugly, before sauntering off with Bambi in tow, her crimped hair bouncing in the wind as she broke into stride.

This was going to be a long case. I could already feel it.

A stepping stone to Mr. Playboy's operating center had been created. Or at the very least, I could flesh out his character and gauge how tough the case was going to be. This part is what made my job interesting. This case was waking me up from the string of boring cases I had been assigned recently. Potentially, it was the most thrilling and potentially momentous call to justice in my career, as it involved a corrupt police department. Scary. Yet I figured I could handle it.

Let the games begin.

I wanted to get in touch with Hawk and quick. *Whose Hawk?* Only the best rogue James Bond I know. Hawk is an assassin, army brat, and sometimes spy. No, that's not his government name. His high-level spy equipment and tracking devices, if I went by my hunches, were going to be a big help for this case. Hawk exclusively took on highly classified cases. Top secret government agency stuff. He has taken down major government spies and possesses a crazy sixth sense. He was the man to have on your side when you needed back-up. Especially a merry band of corrupt police officers. *Or so it was alleged to be.* We were about to find out on that one.

Now, I was talking to you about Robert Elliot, wasn't I? Ok let me take it from the top. This guy was a *known* playboy: girls swooned over him. He's part of the Manhattan baby-faced crew with the flashy Colgate smiles to match. I'd seen the photos. *He was ok, if you liked that type of thing.* Something in his eyes gave way to a more sinister undertone. It gave me chills when I looked at his company website photo. Strangely enigmatic, though. I wondered if that was part of his panty-dropping appeal.

Robert's father was the prior owner of a multi-million-dollar company and a crafty business shark. Some legit business dealings, some less than legit business dealings. The cops only ever seemed to bust him for minor offenses.

Minor tarnish on the Elliot legacy. Word on the street was that Robert's father embezzled millions of dollars through his various companies. My hunch told me Mr. Playboy inherited his father's dirty laundry racket. Mr. Playboy portrayed himself as quite a smart businessman. I went sniffing and conducted further research. Elliot was a people smart, gift-of-the-gab type of guy. A smooth operator. Supported charities, had solid business dealings. Standard cover-ups. Top-ranked in his university debate team. Robert Elliot graduated top of his class from NYU business school in the '90s, with honors.

I scoffed at the thought – *most likely all his assignments were paid off by money-hungry students.* Now here's where it gets interesting. I started to rummage around in the background of a cold case at his university. I got lucky enough to find stellar public records. The sealed records would take some time to retrieve. Especially since I remained in the dark about who protected him. My street sources from prior detective work I'd done confided a little. They spoke of Robert's abilities at persuasion on campus and the underground university drug hustle he founded. The type of hustle where professors were involved and paid off a hefty percentage. Allegedly, one professor had a seizure during a philosophy lecture due to all the drugs. Not long after that, he was listed as a missing person. Police never linked the cases together. He was never found. *What a surprise.* Smelled like rotten catfish to me. I pegged it on my investigation board to look at the details later. A vision board of criminal activity. So far, Robert's picture existed in the center of it: a picture of Robert's father, his known associates, and drawing pins for the haunts Robert was known to frequent. He split his time between New York and L.A. Specifically, Hollywood. I always started with a preliminary background on the perpetrator to get into their heads and make up a psychological profile.

My eyes were peeled on the board in my kitchen with my arms crossed. This guy oozed cockiness. I scanned through the photos I retrieved of him. Danger lurked in those dark eyes. They appeared as if they held pools of family secrets, yet they were equally fascinating. Something I couldn't quite shake settled in my spirit when I looked at them.

Mr. Playboy missed a month's worth of classes around the same time as the professor's death. On top of that, another mysterious event occurred: a student reporter went missing when she started to dig deeper into an increase of drug intake on campus. A massive spate of unexplained drug comas occurred during a short period of time.

In one student paper, she described students as *'walking around like apocalyptic zombies.'* She wrote about this in the summer of 1990. Then she wound up dead, found face down in a fishpond days after the paper was published. Little did she know it would be her last paper run. The autopsy report said "cause of death: overdose" after a bucket-load of cocaine was found in her system. The way she wrote the paper, with such opposition against drugs, didn't match up with the autopsy. The whole report felt off to me. The levels of cocaine in her system were way beyond the excess of what any human being could consume. Were they sure of the levels? What if my client was right about what he said? That the police fudged the report?

Elliot made a living from – no wait – I mean a fortune from weak humans, and their need to fill an empty void with temporary highs and happiness, mainly coke. Escapism was yours, just name your price and poison. Known to the rich and famous for his crazy outlandish house parties, the entry price: millionaire status. He made all his partygoers sign an Non-Disclosure Agreement at the door. My client passed on this information, as he'd witnessed a few of Robert's shindigs.

I certainly didn't have a million dollars. I was a guest of a supermodel, so hopefully I passed. A vanilla wafer compared to this crowd. Don't get me wrong, back in my university days I smoked a joint or two. Just for the experience, and to not feel so left out in my college days. Not really my lane, so I stayed away from it for the most part. I gotta tell you I wasn't always going to be a private investigator. I wanted to be a photographer. I spent a lot of time in darkrooms. Paid off in a way, now my bread and butter clients have me take photos of the bad guys, amongst other things. They were the usual: wife is cheating. I need you to tail her for a couple of days so she can't screw me over in alimony. Husband is working late; can you find out who he's screwing? One lady from the Hamptons paid me six months' salary to tail her husband! The 'amongst other things,' included low-level spy gadgets or special services, depending on the situation. Like the Hamptons client I helped. I gave her a small black device no bigger than the tip of my index finger to insert into her laptop. It allowed her to check her husband's email. My clients' faces were always the same at the end of the investigation. Usually, it confirmed what the client already knew to be true in their heart of hearts. A harrowing timeline of smutty photos put the nail in the coffin. Gut-wrenching disappointment surfaced as the truth hit them right between the eyes. Men and women with crestfallen faces, and lonely tears as I handed over the pity tissues.

"I can't believe this!"

"How could they do this to me?"

"I gave them everything"

"That fucking bastard!"

"That fucking slut!"

"I gave him a child!"

Humanity at its finest hour. These types of cases were like date repellent for me. One major reason for my single status. What a buzzkill. It was refreshing to be able to work on something more high profile where I could put my sleuth skills to the test. Investigation being my forte. Elliot, with your sexy blue eyes, *you're going downnnn*.

2

SARA

♟

Phone ringing. Urgh. The harsh shrill tone vibrated through my eardrums. I bolted awake with one eye scrunched. The sound came from the left. *Left*. Where is it? Dammit. I patted my hand around on the floor, blindly searching for the device making the awful sound before my coffee. I blew my hair out of my face sitting up on the floor. I read the blue screen of my phone. *Hawk.*

"Hey, to what do I owe the pleasure of this early morning call?" I sleepily slurred. Way too early for this. To be exact, 5:30 a.m. My fantastic dream had me sipping piña coladas at a Hawaii beach bar. My flirt game was working a charm on one of the cabana boys. *Damn.*

A familiar throaty chuckle crackled through the phone. "Sleeping Beauty, I got some news for you. You're going to like it." Hawk knew about the case last week. Normally, Hawk was selective on cases, but I was calling in a favor, and he seemed overly receptive to help. Since my marriage to my job held me captive, my ears perked up.

"Do tell!"

"Let's meet at Little Birdy Café. They do the eggs just right there. Besides, it's your turn to shout." I could hear his big grin through the phone.

I rolled my eyes. "You can update me from your end as well."

"Ok, done deal, see ya in half-hour."

I hung my legs over the bed, reluctantly trying to gather myself enough to get to the instant coffee. If I could drip-feed coffee into my veins, I would. It was my main vice. I tried the green tea thing, but it really didn't hold a candle to a smooth espresso. I usually came to life on the second one. Besides instant coffee doesn't count does it?

I had a place in Maywood, New Jersey, a small village about forty minutes out of the hustle and bustle on a good day from downtown New York. A quiet neighborhood where everybody minds their own business. You can walk your dog peacefully without too much hassle. I got the odd wave from Mrs. Darcy as she sat out on the porch, watching people go by. She's harmless: a great neighborhood spy. Sometimes I wondered if I should employ her. If you wanted the gossip, she was the lady to speak to. She had the low-down on every-one. Best be careful: if you suffered from foot in mouth disease, then she became the person to avoid. A real character within herself, Mrs. Darcy was sporting pink hair - I suspected from a lavender rinse gone wrong. She had the same physical characteristics as a bowling ball. Maywood's favorite community watchdog.

I brought a little house there years ago when prices were low. Good move on my part. Prices have damn near skyrock-eted since then. My place was a fixer upper, I must admit. I still had tiles from the 1970's in the kitchen. That age-old, yeah-I'll-get-around-to-it promise I made to myself. A pretty brownstone with the customary stoop of NYC, but with an actual yard. If you were living in the heart of New York this would cost you a grip. Prices went up in height there, not out.

Shoeboxes. Or as real estate agents colorfully named them, the New York Loft. *Not for me.* I needed to spread my wings with a backyard.

Before becoming a kickass private investigator, I worked in a ho-hum job. A photoshop, at least I figured if I couldn't take photos, I could develop other people's. I participated in a few photography shows, but they didn't pan out the way I wanted them to. At that point, I had to get a job to pay bills, right? My boss, Shane, was hopeless with administration, so I gave him a hand at the shop. Shane loved me being there, but there came a point when I started getting restless, craving excitement and wanting more from my dreary life.

At twenty-seven I sat pouting about my life at my favorite coffee shop, until I flicked through the paper. An ad jumped right off the page at me. They were looking for someone to take photos. The assignment was top secret. I had nothing to lose at this point, so I leapt at the chance. Turns out the secret was a man who wanted photos taken of a jackass who he thought to be filing a fraudulent insurance claim. The guy wanted to catch the fraud in the act. The gig promised a handy sum, good for my savings account, back when I was trying to buy my house. That moment cemented my start as a private investigator. Word of mouth grew, and the cases started to trickle in. So much so, I had to let go of my photo lab job with Shane. At thirty-two, I've never looked back.

In my mind, I was the female version of Batman – only smarter, of course. Regular Sara by day, and super-sleuth by night. I rocked this red leather jacket that I bought from a consignment shop. Sort of like my coming-out party as a hot-shot investigator. Nancy Drew eat your heart out. The jacket made me feel badass. I wore it to client meetings sometimes. I always met new clients out at a public location. One, so I could assess them, and see if they were a nutjob. Two, because I didn't want them anywhere near my house. After a couple of cases, I picked up a couple of stalkers for my trouble. I learned the hard way not to reveal my home address. Realistically, if someone wanted to get to me, they could. I was thinking it was probably time to get that downtown office space. Lately, higher stakes investigation cases were starting to come through the door. Like this one…

Time to gather myself and go over the details of the case. *What had Hawk discovered?* What is so new I may have missed it? Admittedly, I needed guidance on this case. My client wanted Elliot stripped bare, since the law wouldn't convict him. He wanted Elliot on his knees eating dirt. He hinted of taking matters into his own hands. I strongly urged him not to do this. He didn't have the firepower that Elliot did. He would wind up floating in the Hudson as well, and *that* wasn't the business.

Nobody, *I mean nobody*, had been able to bust Mr. Playboy. It was the worst kept secret in New York. Too many gaps were in this case for Elliot not to be questioned at least. The Golden Child of criminals continued to skip off into the sunset on his shiny horse. Really got on my last nerve. I gulped down the last of my instant coffee. I headed not too far across town to meet my infamous friend slash sometimes sidekick, Hawk.

Old school classics filled the bustling café. The sound of the coffee machine hissing was the only music I needed to hear. Coffee. Elixir of the gods. Little Birdy Café was a nice, trendy eating spot in Maywood. It was peak coffee hour in the morning, so the corporate crowd were streaming through. Mostly take-away, people were transiting grab and go style on the way to their 9-to-5's.

The waitress shouted out orders: *"Double Macchiato for Sam! Long black for Richard!"* I sighted some of the regulars, and we nodded at each other. Almost like a secret coffee club. Little Birdy had great coffee, and I knew the staff by name. That comes with the territory of living in the Maywood burbs for the last fifteen years. I spotted Hawk with a baseball cap sloped low over his broody eyes. Typical Hawk, he fancied himself as Mr. Invisible, I think, at times. I passed by the tables to the back of the open window café.

Hawk stood six foot two, an imposing figure of raw athleticism and sinewy muscle built from his army days. A mop of dark brown hair and tawny red complexion. Hawk originated from a Native American mother and a white father from Syracuse. What a mix. Strangely, he could make himself seem inconspicuous, yet stand out all at the same time if need be. Handy skill to have. If he wasn't like a brother to me, and not such the broody type, he would be a good catch.

I greeted Hawk with warm enthusiasm. Great to see him. I hadn't laid eyes on him for months. He mentioned his work. Some top-secret case where he had to lay low. Thankfully, he seemed to have enough free time to work with me on my case. Hawk became my trusted ally – someone who I relied upon. The police couldn't be trusted right now. I did have some allies from the New York police department – don't get me wrong. Because of the nature of the case, I didn't know who on the inside I could count on. I had to feel out the situation, plotting the next steps carefully, before I approached the boys in blue.

Hawk and I originally met back on a case I worked three years ago. One of the crazier cases I inherited. Surprise, surprise – it involved an ex-soldier. The girlfriend came to me because she sensed she was being stalked. *Boy, was she right…* Her psychotic soldier boyfriend thought it would be fun to rig an NYC bus. This is a bus she caught on the daily. Didn't think to mix up her routine. She became an easy target for him, all because she decided not to marry him. Might be a few solid reasons as to why she didn't.

In his first Afghan tour, Hawk graduated to bomb specialist level. This is where his skills came in handy. The infamous case ended up plastered all over the NYC news. Lucky, the ex-boyfriend's timing skills were rusty. Hawk narrowly snatched the girlfriend and me off the bus ten seconds before the bomb exploded. *That's a story for another time.* We became fast friends after that. He slid into the role of designated big brother when I needed him to step in. Like this one. Did I stress the level of danger when the cops are insiders? And whoever else Elliot had on payroll? I felt a lot more at ease with Hawk onboard. We settled into the cafe booth, jabbering about the case.

"So how are you going with the intel?" Hawk threw me a challenging grin.

"Well, I got invited to a party at Mr. Playboy's house, so it's off to a good start. I figured I could put a bug in place. Find out what deals he's got going on."

"So that's the alias? Mr. Playboy?" Hawk's mouth curved into a smirk.

"Yep, that's the word on the street. That he's a ladies' man," I confirmed.

"Hmm, a party?" Hawk mused.

"Yes, a drug party. Well, at least I think it's one anyway. This guy is renowned for his wild parties. I have to sign a Non-Disclosure Agreement. His wife sent it through to me today," I added.

Hawk raised his rugged eyebrow. If there was such a thing, Hawk had them. Even his eyebrows looked like they had special forces capabilities. "Yippee, sounds exciting." Hawk replied in a dry tone. "Just don't come calling me to bail you out when you're doped up to the eyeballs – especially in the middle of three girls in the spa. Oh, wait! On second thought, *do* call me when that happens." Hawk let out a wicked chuckle.

"You're such a lame-o." I air-swatted his face light-heartedly.

"You still love me though." Hawk winked. That I did. He was a good egg.

There was some tinkle of amusement from Hawk. He

thought I was an uptight goody two shoes. I wasn't Don Juan like him. To me though, I took my cases seriously. Desperate clients depended on me for justice. They tried other avenues, but nobody could or would help them. I felt like a modern-day hero in a way. Upholding the law and being undercover simultaneously was a delicate tightrope to walk. I had to know when to remove the mask. To see what was real and what was evil. I guess that's what I was worried about. How deep undercover was I willing to go in order to solve this case?

"Yeh I guess so. You saved my life, so I'll give you a pass," I retorted ruefully.

"Well you know me. Never leave a soldier down in the field. It's against the code." Hawk beamed. I changed the subject quickly.

"So, Hawk what's going on. What do you know?" I ventured with enthusiasm.

Hawk grinned, "So, turns out your boy is in some hot water due to a tip-off given about his company for tax evasion. Apparently an old pissed-off employee."

"Hmm... tell me more. Not going to be enough to pin him. He's just going to pay and keep moving. I'm sure that's not the first time he's encountered a tax situation," I replied with skepticism.

"True. Turns out his old nemesis squeaked to me over a couple of drinks. Ok, a shitload of drinks at Dahlias a couple of nights ago. He mentioned Roberts's name, he said the guy was a cold-blooded son of a bitch," Hawk affirmed.

Dahlias. The dive bar of the century, if you asked me. Located near the outskirts of Harlem. God knows why Hawk loved these places. The man loved dark, dingy dungeons, with red velvet seats. I didn't want to speculate what Hawk got up to in his down time. *Ewww*. But...he had an amazing ability to get people to talk. I would give him that much. My mind ticked over the possibilities.

"And what's this guy's M.O.?"

"He's pissed. Him and Robert were about to broker a major deal for a casino. They couldn't see eye to eye, so he hooked up another deal with a Hong Kong consortium behind his back. This deal was worth a nice sum, apparently."

"Wow, so he just blurted that out right at the bar, huh?" I stared at Hawk for clarity.

"What can I say, people like talking to me, Sara." Hawk shrugged his massive shoulders and faced his palms out in front of him.

"Hawk, *spill*."

"Ok, ok, just so happens this dude is a link to another case that I'm working on. After a few drinks, he decided to give me the down low about this deal with your... Playboy? That's what we're calling him right? Do I get extra brownie points now?" Hawk winked mischievously.

"Nope. Not unless you tell me what you're working on, and how you got that guy to talk." Worth a try.

"Highly classified bluebell. You know the code. And you don't want to know."

I sighed. One day I would catch Hawk slipping, and he would give me some of his trade spy secrets.

"But our cases are linked now. You gotta give me something!" I raised my hands in an exasperated tone.

"No can-do, kiddo. I'm protecting you as well." He winked at me.

Hawk, in his current capacity, acted as a highly trained contract spy/assassin who had been poached by the Secret Intelligence Service (SIS) in Britain. Hawk covered cases that would render a mere mortal a shriveling mess. His mode: cool, calm, collected and hella sharp. He called it his Hawk senses. His grandfather was full-blood Cherokee. Hawk lived on a reservation with him for a while, learning the ways of his tribe. Oh, and did I mention he could wield a tomahawk as well? Not the guy to be messed with. I swear, the guy was psychic as well. The way he sensed things was uncanny. Ran in the bloodline as far as I knew.

"I heard there is a major drug deal going down with some Columbian friends of Robert's," Hawk said casually as he dug into his eggs. My ears perked up like a dog waiting for its afternoon treats. I learned over the years to trust Hawk's sources, but still: how the hell did he get this information? No point asking him – he wouldn't tell me. That much I knew. Funny how he left the juicy parts until the end of the conversation. "Thought you might like that one."

I swiped at him again. "I'm so sick of you!" He ducked like the expert he was.

"The name is Marcus Suarez. Leader and pioneer of one of Columbia's first major drug cartels. Right now, him and Robert are besties," he continued as he devoured the last of his eggs.

My mind kicked into high gear. Was this guy linked further back? Could he have been linked to the university drug hustle? Could I solve two cases in one? My ambition started to kick in. I listened with investigative intent.

"How long have they been connected?" I responded.

"A few years, according to my source – but could be earlier. I don't have the exact date," Hawk added. "Keep an eye or ear out if you hear about this guy at the party. They are probably going to try and sample some new product to their high-end customers before they seal the deal. Know what I mean?"

"Yeh, I know what you're saying. So, they're in business?" I asked draining the last of my coffee.

"Yeh, they have a deal going down," Hawk answered. "Let me know if you need any further intel on this guy."

"Will do. Operational expansion, you think? Elliot has never been busted for operating a drug ring."

"It's pretty much like an open secret to those in the know, though. Elliot has paid to keep a lot of people quiet – that's why. For sure, it's some sort of expansion going on. Plus, the Columbians have a higher grade of coke. We're talkin' international here. If anyone could pull it off, it would be Mr. Moneybags." Hawk arched an eyebrow at me.

"Ok, so you think he's smuggling coke into the country?" I questioned.

"High possibility. Just where, and how?" Hawk countered.

"I'm trying to work out where Michael Sawyer fits in. If he's a user or not. Seemed like a pretty clean-cut guy to me. Tech guy. Working in software development. I'm not seeing the link yet?"

I nodded my head with the realization that this case was a whole lot bigger than I thought. Note to self: I voluntarily signed up for this life. *Sheesh.*

"Hmm. I don't think it's going to take long to see the correlation. Elliot has his hand in everything." Hawk's brow furrowed as he chomped on his spinach. "My guy in the Narcs division said something strange about drug overdoses in the Hamptons, Harlem, and the Bronx. Plus, links to Hollywood. They're trying to get names right now, but nobody's snitching. Someone has a firm hold on them even with generous plea deals. No squawkers so far."

"Huh," I replied. Sounded fishy to me.

"Sure you don't need me to run some more intel for you? This guy is dangerous, kid, so keep your wits about you and stay sharp. This is not a drill. Stay connected," Hawk warned.

"Gotcha." My head began the process of formulating a sequence of puzzle pieces that might bring this case together. Early days yet. When I met the guy, I would see more. Time to get to work. Weird. Same pattern as the overdoses in the university hustle from what Hawk told me. Only this time, it sounded like Elliot was upgrading to improve his services.

"Sara, don't say I didn't warn you, though. Mr. Playboy is smooth with the ladies. Apparently, this guy is so slick, he literally melts women's panties off," Hawk spoke coolly.

I scoffed. "I'm a professional, Hawk, and you know how I roll." I pointed to myself with mock importance. I was such an awkward weirdo sometimes. To be honest, I harbored some nervousness about meeting the guy.

Hawk smiled that slow smile of his. It was irritating me at this point. Like he knew something I didn't. "Well here's the thing: I know you're not dating right now."

"*What*? I date! I just haven't told *you* about it. Mind your business…"

Hawk reached over and ruffled my hair a little. "Thou dost protest too much." He waggled his finger at me. I sunk my teeth into my cherry and chocolate muffin with mock disgust.

"Do yourself a favor and listen to my warning. He is going to eat you alive otherwise. Women are chomping at the bit for this dude. Even though he's got that bad ass model by his side. I don't know why the hell she married that dick."

Hawk's eyes clouded over when he mentioned this chick's name. At the time, I didn't think too much of it. Just a little frustration that a hot supermodel was bagged by a sleazy womanizing criminal. Truth be told, when I saw the pictures of Mr. Playboy, they gave me a rush. Elliot was becoming more intriguing, the more I found out. Hawk broke my secret train of thought.

"So, your cover is at Vogue with this supermodel, right?"

"Yeh, she's super bratty. I'm not looking forward to it." I peeled the bottom layer of my muffin off and kept eating.

"You sound like you know her? Do you know her, Hawk?"

"No," Hawk shrugged. "Just from the magazines… She in love with this dick?"

Odd question… but I answered. "I think she's in over her head, and likes the lifestyle he provides for her. That's my observation on first take. Oh, and the parties, of course."

Why was Hawk so inquisitive about this supermodel? I

met the chick once. *Maybe just trying to get an overview on the case.*

"Why do you ask? I didn't take you to be the supermodel type?" I gave a sneaky smile of my own.

"You gotta crush I don't know about? I can hook you up. She's going to be there with Mr. Panty Dropper though." I cackled at the thought. What a mess that would be. I always imagined Hawk to be way too rogue for that. Seemed to be more into the femme fatale type.

I kept going. "Sorry. She likes billionaire bad boys. You're fresh out of luck."

Little did Sara know how small the world was...

3

HAWK

S triking blonde. Legs for days, glistening crystal white smile with a cute gap in her teeth. Pale porcelain skin so delicate it almost looked like it would crack. Sweet oriental perfume. I was kicking back in my apartment after meeting Sara, reminiscing about the time I met this beautiful gazelle.

We bumped into each other at a launch party. My mission covered a stake out for a rich client overseas with ties to the British government. A glitzy shebang. *Bullshit*. One of those slick, polished events at the Grand Hyatt. Fancy chandeliers, bright lights and walking egos in tuxedos. I was there with a job to do. Supreme focus on my mark for the night. Surveillance at this stage. 12′ o'clock. Mmm. Cute giggly blonde, unusual looking, red nails and set of pins I imagined wrapped tightly around me. A light formed around her almost like a halo, I swear. They had some spotlight circling the venue, and it happened to land on this gorgeous critter as I looked over. A sign from God. She *was* beautiful. I refocused in. I had to remember the mark. So, I parked the erotic thoughts about her. I could recount our meeting that night without having to strain my memory.

I scanned the room, setting eyes on my mark, watching his movements, stalking him. Earlier, I had bugged the ballroom. I was ready to rumble. I listened in on the conversation the mark started. This part of the gig was boring to me. Still necessary. Pity, I was going to have to break this guy's neck later. But, hey, them's *the breaks*. I chuckled to myself - internal joke. I would save that one for Sara. She would love it. *Assassin jokes.* Had to be there. I held the statuesque blonde in my peripheral the whole night. Our paths didn't cross until a little later in the evening.

She stood in a semicircle with one other girl with thick curly hair. She was cute, slightly smaller in height, and Afro American. By the looks of her, probably a model. Plus, some hipster dude that looked like a Poindexter. Boredom covered her face. I smiled; *I knew a way to make her un-bored*. I flashed her a slow, sexy smile when she glanced in my direction. She winked back at me, mouthing hello. She rolled her eyes to indicate how drab the event was. I flashed back to my task quickly as static filled my ears...

"Rich... I thought I told you to lay low. Now's not the time to be cutting deals. Things are too hot right now, we've got McCarthy in our back pocket, and there's no guarantee, you know."

Another guy chimed in. "Yeah, I hear you, but we gotta hot deal that's not going to come across our table for some time. We gotta make moves... Are you in or out?"

Looky, looky, the fire was starting again. McCarthy, the dirty ass cop protecting pieces of shit to make a lousy buck. *Thank you for making my night.* This line of work made my life. I'd crossed paths with so many dirty cops in this city, it wasn't funny. Especially when working for the Brits. You see, I straddled both sides of the fence when I wanted to. If I ever got busted, it would be classed as high treason. I would be locked in the New York sewers and fed to the rats before I saw the light of day again. They would torture me. What can I say? I'm a guy who likes to live on the edge. Plus, those Brits paid a lotta money. I wasn't loyal to the U.S. More like ambivalent. A lot of shit went down in my early army days. Deliberate sabotage by American government officials. These days, I handled the likes of extortion, embezzlement, drugs, murders – that type of thing of late. Standard procedure for my private, high-end clients. Longer cases involved me *sometimes* being a spy. Yup, a spy for the Secret Intelligence Unit in Britain (SIS) Freelance.

I picked up more information across the airwaves.

"Yeah, I'm in."

Baldy had a grim look on his face, his eyes darting nervously around the building. They split and went their separate ways. I couldn't get a read on the other guy; I only saw the back of his neck. I noticed he had a small triangle on the base. I locked this in my mind's treasure chest for later. I pressed a small device in my breast pocket, and it clicked. Nobody knew it was a camera that could shoot at high zoom capacity through clothing, and underwater. A little something extra I picked up from my Brit intelligence colleagues. I would scan the pics for reading later.

Now that that was outta the way...

I diverted my attention back to the long-legged blonde hottie. I craned my neck to the left... she'd split. *Dayum*. My left shoulder became warm with body heat. The kind when you know somebody is standing nearby. The blonde hottie was beside me, in eye view distance.

I sidled up to the makeshift drinks station that overlooked the dance floor. Her left elbow grazed my ribcage as I turned to face the blonde.

"Ooo, sorry." She blushed.

"I'm not." Insert slow smile, Hawk style.

The chemistry between us was red hot. Electricity pulsed through the air. Like you could reach out and touch it. Like a live wire. She looked at me squarely in the face. Freckles made themselves barely visible underneath her makeup. *Adorable.* Gave her a down to earth appeal. I was surprised. I liked surprises. She smirked.

"Cute. I haven't seen you around the scene... What are you doing here?"

"Oh, really? What scene is that?" I was amused at this point. Pure sass. I could respect it.

"The modelling charade you're looking at." She gestured with her long slender arm around the ballroom, slightly intoxicated. "I wondered if you were a model as well."

"Nope. I was invited." That's all I said. Need to know basis only. Nice to keep some mystery.

"Oh, do tell." The cute blonde seemed entertained. I looked past her slightly, seeing if there was any sign of the mark re-entering the building, and surveying the scene.

"If I tell you, I would have to kill you." I replied with a straight face.

The model raised an eyebrow and giggled. I would never kill an innocent civilian – that wasn't my style. I knew some assassins who had no qualms about it. Especially if one got in the way of their operation. But that was neither here nor there. The model stared at me, tilting her head. I was close enough to her to take in her heady scent: a mixture of jasmine and vanilla. An unusual oriental smell that added to her sexiness. Models weren't my type. We really didn't have so much in common. I mean, I'm not sure how they related to me being in Berlin throwing hand grenades from a rooftop... *But this woman.* She had me mesmerized. I admired her boldness. We looked at each other for what seemed like an eternity, but what was really only five seconds, max. "*Sooo...*" I disintegrated the code of silence.

"My place or yours?" she cooed. I raised an eyebrow. Two

reasons for that statement: extreme confidence or drunkenness. I read her body's energy, and her face. She was serious.

"How about we start with a name first?"

"Minor detail. My name's Evana." She replied in a silky tone. "What's yours?"

"Hawk."

"Hawk, huh? Sounds like a fun time with you." I scanned her thoroughly with a smile.

I'm plenty fun, babe, don't you worry about that.

"How about we meet tomorrow or Wednesday for lunch?"

"Wow!" Evana imitated surprise. "Like a daytime thing?"

"Yes, I like to talk to my women first."

Evana shot me a toothy-gapped grin. "That's all I meant. To talk… just… ah… at my house. Not likely that I'm your woman, though. I'm not one of those." More little flirty games from the blonde seductress. "I figured you for a wham-bam man." She stroked my jaw with one slender finger. I grinned, looking around her. Still on the job. No sign that the mark had re-entered. I relaxed a little.

"No, I like my women coherent."

She had no idea. I already had sweet plans for her. I wanted her to be mine. Didn't take me long to decide. Evana reached into her purse. She pulled out a cherry red lipstick and grabbed my arm. I carefully wrote my digits.

"I don't carry my phone on nights like this. People have snatched it and sold my private photos to paparazzi. Can you believe it!" She threw both hands up in disbelief and drunkenness. I heard footsteps coming our way and looked up.

"*Evana! Evana!*" Her friends gave her a smug, *you're doing that again, aren't you?* look.

The connection between us felt like firelight. All the other women were shadows I left in the night. I couldn't hold down a relationship. Not with my job. Too much at stake. I mean, I had to dodge the work question often enough. I couldn't tell anyone about my cases. Too much risk. So, it became a series of lies I told. That in itself was a nightmare. I adopted a love 'em and leave 'em attitude, when deep down I really wanted to tell someone. I wanted to share my life. But, it had to be the right one I told.

The daytime date came. We were sitting across from waterfront views. Her place overlooked Gantry State Park in Long Island City. The leggy blonde lived there rent-free. A present, courtesy of Vogue magazine. A racy red dress molded brilliantly to her body with the back cut out. I liked it. I could reach her skin to skin with my hand. Smoldering black eyeliner made her eyes look feline. The rest of her face laid bare. She might have had one layer of make-up, but it wasn't noticeable. Clear lip gloss. Her hair hung down past her shoulders. Long slender pins, sexy ankle-strapped stilettos in the color black. *My favorite.* Her perfume smelled different from the last one, distinctly like peaches combined with musk. A warm kiss on the cheek from her. Lips like melted butter touched my face. She was fresh off a photo shoot.

"Hi, hot stuff. Glad you could make it."

That was the beginning of the end for me. The leggy model started to maneuver her way into my heart. Something I thought would never happen. The love affair began intensely for us from the start. *Blissful*. Falling into one another. The blonde's legs wrapped around me, just like I envisioned. Furious love-making of the best kind. I worked my cases during the day, slipping in and out at night as needed. I didn't waver. I was laser sharp when I was work-ing, but I found myself softening with her. She subdued my defenses a little bit. Not all the way, but enough so my vulner-abilities were exposed. She didn't question me so much. A refreshing change from all the other nosey women. It allowed me to keep the affair going. I didn't know how long it would last, though.

Sometimes, she was so focused on her modeling gigs that it was easy for me to sidestep questions. Eventually, she started to assess my movements differently. She would ask questions about how I talked in code on the phone.

"Who were you talking to just now? Why did you call him a beaver?"

"No reason, just a silly name." She started to ask if we could catch up with my friends. Not just hers.

"You know I've never met your friends. You've met mine. Feels kinda strange to me. We should invite them out."

"They're pretty busy people. They're usually not free for weeks or months at a time…"

Normal questions and pace for someone new you're dating. She wanted to know my life… I wanted her to stop them. *The questions, that is.* This is where the unraveling started. We began to get into little bickering arguments. She started going out more as an act of rebellion. Thoughts festered in my mind about having a serious relationship with her. I wanted to tell her about my world - but I had to be able to trust her wholeheartedly. A real relationship with a woman. I was entertaining this new territory for the first time in my life. Trying to carefully see how, and if, it was possible and functional. Insert high-level espionage cases. Shady, Hollywood connections – that to me, screamed impossible. What if the cat got outta the bag one night when she was drunk? It would bring unnecessary drama, possibly dead bodies, and a world of pain.

I couldn't pinpoint the feelings that made her different from my other lovers. Probably if I did, I wouldn't be with her. They had been nice girls too. It was like some love bug had snuck up from behind and snuffed me. Like a street king hit. *I was in love.* Evana was like an insatiable weakness. I didn't do models. Those cute freckles she kept hidden did me in. Made her look innocent when she wasn't wearing makeup. Her laughter, and the deeper conversations we had about the world at large. She was smart, and intuitive. She had many complex layers to her. For all her partying ways, she had a whole other side. Maybe that borderline obsession in me had overstayed its welcome. Who fucking knows? *But it sure felt good*. I prayed time would pass, and the aching feeling in my chest would subside.

4

SARA

♟

Flash on, flash off, flash on, flash off. Ten-second intervals in flash and permanent eye damage from overpriced strobe lighting. *Thank you very much.* I could see the inside lights from meters away. I made my way up to the mahogany doors with pale blue glass inserts. I looked closer, realizing the glass inserts had diamonds wedged into them. *What in the world?* I shook my head in disbelief. If you told me, and I didn't see it with my own eyes, I wouldn't have believed you. This guy had Liberace-ish tastes, and then some. *Strange*, given that Robert fitted a completely different profile in my brain. I thought he might be a clean contemporary lines type of guy. The penthouse type, you know.

Evana opened the door wearing bright fuchsia lipstick, bronzed cheekbones, a high slicked back ponytail and long falsies – obviously channeling Bridget Bardot. Cloaked in white, she resembled a Grecian goddess with her dress clinging to all the right places. A dead ringer for a female character straight out of *Miami Vice*. I heard the show's theme music running riot in my head. This gorgeous chameleon could master any style and look. No wonder she was NYC's hottest model right now. I gazed at her with admiration. She stared at me with slightly more approval than our first meeting at the bar. *Ok, ok, I was doing better.*

My choice was a powder blue A - line dress with one shoulder out. A big step up for me. I used the cheat code and watched Anna Wintour's documentary on fashion and style. She represented a real force to be reckoned with in the fashion industry. Maybe she was the muse behind *The Devil Wears Prada*. A smile or two wouldn't hurt the lady, though. *Yeesh.* One of her quotes stuck with me.

"You either know fashion or you don't." Well I sure as hell didn't, but for the validity of this case, I had to become actress of the year and learn. Maurice loaned me the dress from wardrobe on the first day. You could say I was on a steep uphill fashion curve.

"Hunny, if you're going to do this, we need you to Vogue it up! At least look the part!" Maurice was charming, fashionable, and gay. He had given me a large manual to read, all about fashion and the expectation of Vogue interns. Not like I wanted to deal with all of this. Maybe I would get used to it. It just might be something new and exciting for me. I straightened my hair for a change. I made the effort, and it turns out I didn't look half bad. Just a smidge of mascara swiped across my lashes to enhance them. Clear gloss smeared across my lips. I'm a minimalist - even the gloss was a stretch for me. I didn't want anything sticking to my face. I always wondered about wearing sticky gloss on a hot summer's day. What if gnats got stuck to your lips? What if you were talking to a hot guy, and all these swarming gnats made a beeline to your lips? Maybe, because of the gloss, thinking it was nectar? A gal's worst nightmare. This is where my brain went to. It's not pretty there sometimes. A bunch of weird and abnormal thoughts.

Back to my shoes...

Well, they were my go-tos, my trusty, black velvet wedges. Ankle straps that were for practical reasons as much as sexiness. I knew I could still run in them and kick some serious ass. In the past, I've needed to make a quick exit or two. I know for certain they're the best shoes for the job.

Evana gave me a closed smile. "I see you got some help from Maurice." She ushered me in with one hand as she casually leaned against the doorframe. I tried not to slap her in my mind. Outwardly, I flashed her back the same small smile. I stepped onto a cold, sleek, white marble floor. The place opened out to a large open living space as soon as I walked in. Wow. Luxury. Class. Status. Seduction. His home embodied it all. I scanned my eyes around the room. The balcony staircase had more marble in it than a Greek statue. A massive fish tank stood to my left. An array of tropical fish and lobster swam back and forth, going nowhere fast. *Cliché.* Humans of all assortments, everywhere. The room reeked of money, fame, sex, and celebrity status. The who's who in the zoo were there.

"Do you have a phone?" Evana quipped.

"Yes, I do."

"Give it up." She signaled with her manicured hand to pass over my phone.

"Why?" I knew why but still wanted to hear her answer.

"Confidentiality. People come to Robert's parties to be free without restraint. All the celebs are here. They want to remain anonymous. And you have the signed Non-Disclosure Agreement? Recognize anyone?"

"A few, yeh." I slid the signed document over to her. *Dammit.* I hoped to keep my phone. Luckily, I had a few tricks up my sleeve.

I took note of the B-grade soap stars that filled the space. I recognized faces from *Days of Our Lives*. Wonders never ceased. I remember growing up watching Stefano and

Marlena on the show. That guy never wanted to die. You could watch it, and six months later the same situation continued to play out. I only know this because I broke my arm years back. I was cooped up feeling sad and sorry for myself on the couch. I *might* have developed a mild soap addiction to *Days of Our Lives* reruns. *Don't judge me, ok?* It wasn't my finest hour.

I handed over my phone to Evana. She placed it on the top shelf of the cupboard in a clear glass bowl. If there were keys in there I was going to freak out. From what I could see it was just a bunch of cell phones. Phew. No swingers allowed.

"You get it back when you leave."

"Ok."

Two women in front of us were slung over the back of a super expensive-looking couch. Their voices sounded like high-pitched hyenas. They were high as kites. Seconds later, their tongues were dancing together. Champagne glasses with gold bottoms were clasped in their hands. Handsome men with no shirts on, chest-bumping or rather chest sliding down one another... I adjusted my eyes to what I knew I was about to witness. *Debauchery*. Not that I had any aversion to this. Their chests were nice. But it was sort of weird. *Ecstasy*. Culprit found. Snow white powder, glass tables, short straws, credit cards, pills of all colors and sizes were on the table. It was on for young and old. Odd that a stranger like me would be granted access to this crazy world. Maybe it was a rite of passage for models from Vogue. An expectation that this is just what went on in the modelling world.

Speaking of this… Out of the corner of my eye I made out two people humping pot plants. I didn't move my head to look. My mind gravitated to sizing up the room, and its occupants. *Roberts's office... where was it?* I maintained my composure amongst the madness. Music pumped through the speakers with enough bass to make your chest rise and fall. Some techno number I'd never heard of. Evana appeared unfazed by it all. *What had I stepped into?* The whole scene was like a gigantic twisted circus gone wrong.

"What's your poison, Ms. Sara? Are you drinking or partaking in a li'l white Christmas with me?" She smiled seductively.

I gave her a grim smile. "No Christmas for me. I will have a glass of champagne, though." I craved something to keep me centered from all this over-stimulation.

"Oh phooey, you're no fun." She faked a fed-up look at me. Seems she forgot my question at the bar about getting a stash. If I could get my hands on a sample of coke, I could trace it. I leaned in and whispered to Evana,

"Know where I can get a sample though for later? Who can I contact?"

"I can always get you a stash." Confusion washed over her face, she frowned at the question since I wasn't about to use right now. That would be too easy. I wanted her to admit her husband was the ringleader. While Evana retrieved our drinks, I kept taking a poll on the surroundings. I looked up beyond the staircase. I saw what looked to be two rooms on the right. *Hmm, one of those might be Robert's office...*

Evana left me standing at a glass table where people had dumped their bags. Didn't Elliot have a cloakroom here? *Strange. But then again, the whole party was next level weird.* Scary in a way, because I couldn't anticipate what would happen next. Coke coated the glass table near me. People were standing around the table, talking nonchalantly. As if they weren't standing in front of a glass table with coke on it. I glanced into the deep corners of the room. I searched for in-house cameras. None in my eye line. Didn't mean there weren't any. I knew Robert kept cameras in his house. Had to. Being a strategic risk taker, I decided to pull out a piece of double-sided tape from my purse. I discreetly stuck it to the powder on the table with my thumb. I looked around to make sure nobody witnessed. Too busy talking. Good. I placed the tape inside a slip pocket of my purse for sampling. Hawk would be able to decipher the details. He had a narcotics detection unit that could run a trace. Don't ask me how he organized access to that unit. There were many grey areas to Hawk's mode of operation. I wanted to determine how high grade the coke was.

I refocused my attention back to the party as I waited for Evana to return with the bubbles. People were dancing, drinking, and openly doing drugs. Exchanges of pills were happening, mouth to mouth. I penetrated the crowd for information. My mind started to calculate how to sneak upstairs to the office. As soon as I thought my plans were coming together, I was interrupted. I swiveled my head to the right, sighting the object of my disruption. A shot of pure-fire adrenalin circuited through my system from head to toe. My head reeled so fast, I had to blink my eyes rapidly to shake it off.

The man who hunted women. Everything in his stride spoke of it. Never mind his baby face.

Robert Elliot. *Holy shit.* I struggled to catch my breath. *Ok, breathe Sara, keep your head.* I prayed he wouldn't sense my reaction. This guy oozed with the undertone of violence and raw masculine power.

Crisp white shirt, slightly open at the top, a clean fresh linen scent wafted through my nose. *What was that?* Three o'clock shadow, muscular lean build, not too much. Just right. Navy blue slacks. Diamond cufflinks. Dark chestnut hair, and cool blue eyes that resembled jagged icebergs. You could drown in those icy depths. I cast my gaze away, as he pierced me with his. He resembled a sleek and silent tiger as he approached. A simple smile. Sexy, seductive, and cheeky rolled into one.

"And to whom do I owe the pleasure of your presence?" A dry high-pitched cough left my lips. I sounded very much like a wounded chipmunk. Where was the hole to shrink into when you needed it? These intense feelings surfacing in me couldn't be possible. Especially not for this guy.

"Oh, hi." I held out a stiff hand; very formal. An attempt to put ample distance between me and him. My last date was with a retired cop. He wanted to take me on a fishing date with his buddies. *No thanks.* Probably should have taken him up on it. He seemed a lot safer than this guy, now that I thought about it.

"I'm a new colleague of your wife. My name's Sara. She invited me tonight." He seemed highly amused by my nervousness.

"Uh-huh. You're the one she was talking about. Nice to meet you. You work at Vogue, right?"

He took my hand, kissing it. Pure heat from his lips blazed through my forearm, right to my shoulders. It hit my brain like a Mac truck. I pulled it away fast. Like a kid who just touched a hot stove. His fiery energy diffused through me. Those iceberg eyes skimmed me up and down as if to undress me. He stepped closer. I caught his scent of pure masculine energy. *Back off, dude.* He wasn't intoxicated or under the influence, like the partygoers. He was stone-cold sober, from what I observed. Simply entertaining his wayward clients. I glanced quickly in the direction he came from. Three men in suits were seated. They, too, appeared to be relatively sober. One fitted the description of being Columbian. The other two looked to be from U.S. shores. I didn't have time to garner a better read on the situation, because the man-god stood in front of me. *Wait.* I mean killer, *and* husband.

"Right. I do," I replied, shifting from foot to foot uncomfortably. He possessed a raw, innate power that unnerved me, putting me off balance. Yet, I remained glued to the spot. I was unable to excuse myself from speaking to him. He whispered a little too close to my ear. So close, his bottom lip grazed my earlobe. I yanked my head away sharply and frowned.

"And, where is my stunning wife? Do you know?" He put his hand on the small of my back as he said it. *Power play.* A heat pad of fingertips lit up my back. The whispers of his voice floated like a lullaby through my eardrums. I angled my foot to the left to move away from him, so he wasn't standing so close. I could then gain my equilibrium and have his hand slip away from me.

"Ah -" before I could finish, Evana came up behind Robert with drinks in tow. She had a sparkly spaced out look on her face. She'd been gone a few minutes longer than it took to grab a drink. I put two and two together. I guessed that she had been taking a bathroom break with an illegal substance. 'White Christmas' as it was referred to with her circus mates. At least I was safe from Elliot's clutches for now. I gave a silent sigh of relief as the attention diverted to Evana. Robert seemed annoyed, a stern glower crossed his face so quick I didn't know if it happened or not. I watched his body stiffen as he read her. Evana, oblivious to his frustration, kissed him on the cheek.

"Hi, babe! So, you met my friend Sara... isn't she cute?" Evana handed me a glass of champagne with a gold bottom on it. Fancy schmancy.

"Yeh, she really is." Robert's eyes bored through me once again. I'm sure my cheeks flushed red. Evana grinned with a dopey look on her face. She was totally out of it.

"Maybe, you could hook her up with one of your friends, Robert?" she added playfully, touching Robert's nose.

Robert laughed out loud. *Yikes!* He had the husky laugh of the devil's spawn.

"Somehow, Sara's tastes strike me as being more refined. She needs a real man." His blue eyes hooded over, as if he was staring right inside my soul.

No filter. Evana danced a few meters away, floating to the breeze of the music. No fucks given. Her long, slender arms waving back and forth like a tree. What a scene. This moment reminded me of being naked in a shopping mall. I had that dream once, and it was terrifying. Yet, here I was reliving it in the flesh. Maybe the dream was a premonition of what was to come.

"I'm completely fine, and happily single." I managed to squeak the sentence of untruth out.

Evana grinned and broke out of her dancing trance. She grabbed me by the arm, and left Robert standing, watching intently with his cool baby blues.

Robert eventually walked to a corner with other men sipping on a brown liquid. Not so sober. *Hennessy?* Two security guards were at the door keeping watch. They seemed to be enjoying the show, nodding to one another every few minutes with a smirk.

I took Elliot for a Hennessy drinker, smooth – like he was. His muscular legs were crossed, a faint smile on his sexy lips. So far, I managed to stay incognito from other partygoers. They were in their cliques. I wondered if he was thinking about how fucked up all these people were. That he had a hand in making all of it manifest. The Columbian in the group could be the man Hawk spoke of. *Was it the foreign connect?* My investigative mode paused and as Elliot saw me looking back, our eyes locked. I felt a shiver go through me. His eyes were deathly cold. Like he knew I was an imposter. I shifted my feet again, grabbing my throat nervously. He winked in reply and turned back to the group of Columbian men. How did he do that? *He busted me!* Shit. Had to be more careful next time.

Stay focused, Sara. You shouldn't be thinking of what this handsome hunk looks like with his clothes off. Those website photos were no match for his presence in person. Animal magnetism and power can't be experienced through the screen, I found out.

"I'm taking you on the grand tour!" I think I just creamed

my pants from wanton desire. Evana was too high to notice my demeanor.

A grand ballroom palace. As we reached closer to the staircase, I realized the marble banisters had a circular emblem engraved on them. Robert C. Enterprises. The family dynasty from hell. As we climbed, I noticed the men and women hanging off the railings. Talking, drinking, kissing, and seducing one another in dark corners. I heard moans coming from behind closed doors, the closer we got to the top of the stairs. So many rooms and doors in the place made my head swirl.

Meanwhile, the music rocked through my system along with the bubbles. In combination, it made me feel flighty. I hadn't eaten much, and my senses had taken a beating. I needed to fill my stomach with something.

"He's a hottie, huh?" Evana broke my thoughts. *Was that a trick question?*

"I mean - he's alright if that's what you like. He's your husband, after all."

I felt my throat clench as I squawked out the answer. She blew out a dreamy laugh.

"Cut the crap. Women practically lose their shit over him. It's ok. I know." Evana slanted her eyes at me. I smiled weakly at her as we headed up the enormous Liberace-looking staircase.

"He's not what people think. I warn you." Her voice held a knowing tone that might hold clues to the case. This is the reason I came to the party in the first place.

"Why would you warn me? He's *your* husband," I countered. The moans got louder as we planted our feet at the top of the stairs. I raised my eyebrows in curiosity. I could only imagine what was going on behind closed doors.

"When I met him, he was a ladies' man. It's not like I don't know his rep. He comes home to me, so that's what matters."

It sounded like it more than mattered. *A whole lot.* A little more juice for the case. No real surprises so far.

"What do people think about Robert?" I asked calmly, hoping to keep Sara comfortable enough to keep jabbering.

"Oh, just things... and heard stuff, but he looks after me, you know? I have everything I need, so I don't say anything." Her eyes were glazed over, and the hard edge I'd been met with at the club completely dissolved.

"Hmm." I didn't want to get her off guard, so I didn't press her. She would reveal more as the night went on, I figured.

"I really am more pissed about this stupid ex of mine. I wish I could get over him. Don't tell Robert I said that." She spoke in a hushed tone. "He sent me a message to say hello last week, that's all."

"Oh really? What happened with that?" If I was going to be babysitting the supermodel, might as well find out the inner workings of her mind. Freudian slips could provide vital details for the case.

"He was always so cagey when we were together. It was like he had a double life or something. He's texting, and calling me even now. He knows I'm with Robert. I just hope Robert doesn't find out, otherwise I'm dead. Literally."

"Robert would never harm you, would he?" A presumptuous answer sunk into my brain. I knew the outcome subconsciously.

Evana panicked like she shouldn't have said anything. She burped from the champagne bubbles, and started giggling nervously. "Oops, I drank a little too much."

Now, I pressed her: "Robert would never hurt you, would he?"

Evana glanced sideways at me, her eyes were still dopey from the drugs.

"He's a very powerful man. Don't be fooled by his good looks, Sara." Her eyes widened for emphasis.

"Are you scared of him, Evana?" I inquired with concern.

"Like I said, he can be intimidating. But he has plenty of money, and I'm a hot fucking model. What more could I ask for, really?" Another drug-induced giggle escaped as she raised her arms high in the air. *So, Robert threatened her?* She didn't give me a straight answer. This guy needed to be put behind bars. My judgement call was made. Somehow, I couldn't see him locked in a prison cell.

From what I saw downstairs, coke was still in fashion. I observed all the coke being rolled up in dollar bills, and passed around the table like sugar. I thought that drug went out in the 90's, and pills were in? My theory had been smashed to smithereens since entering Robert's lair.

We reached the upstairs level. The first door on the right of the staircase was Robert's office, as I suspected. My goal; to distract Evana long enough to put a bug device underneath the table. Even though as a private investigator in NYC it was illegal. All bets were off in this case. From the time I entered the party I had reasonable cause for a search warrant. The drugs were in plain view. Corrupt cops and civilians were on payroll, so the usual methods didn't apply. I had to get a little dirty with this one. The laws stated if Robert was in a public place, I could record him there. Or at least within the distance of the telephone. I was willing to stretch the truth like a rubber band on this one. The device I was using had no distance limit. Of course, Hawk had gifted me with one of his many gadgets. We entered the office and I pretended to look around nonchalantly. Evana stood in the corner, starry eyed. She was none the wiser to me casing the office.

I did a quick scan: photocopier, papers, filing cabinet right-hand corner, large bay window with a view to the street. A paperweight stood out on the right-hand side of the desk. Very orderly, more mahogany wood. An uber-masculine power office, smelling deeply of musk...

Hmm, I wondered what it would be like to be his secretary. On that desk. Shut up, Sara! Get it together.

Water glass on the right of the desk. Half full. Cognac in a decanter to the left, near his mahogany bookcase. Books about business, law and human psychology filled the shelves. *The Art of War* included. Either he had sociopathic tendencies or was highly strategic, which made a lotta sense. Paperweight. *That's it!* A lotus flower made of glass stood out to me. The feminine touch in his office stood out like a sore thumb to me. I picked it up and pretended to admire it. The bug devices these days were extremely small, and barely visible. This one happened to be see through. The same color as the glass of the paperweight.

"Wow, this is nice." I let the glass slide over my fingers, as I determined the best placement for the device.

"That paperweight is from Robert's ghastly mother. That woman is a nightmare on two legs." Evana shuddered as if she was present in the room.

"Oh, really? It's quite pretty." I pressed the device to the bottom of it with my palm, so Evana couldn't tell what I was doing. I set it back down on the desk.

"Yes, well Robert seems to like it. She's the matriarch of the family. Doesn't like me at *all*."

"Why?" I swung around to look at her.

"Oh, I don't know. Says I'm not from the right bloodline. Some bullshit like that." Evana waved me off like she didn't want to talk about it.

Interesting. *Was Elliot ruled by his mother?* I didn't respond. Meanwhile, step one in my plan was complete. I swept my eyes over the office. I made a mental note of the filing cabinet, and the placement of the computer. *If I ever had the opportunity...* My eye picked up a navy-blue blazer hanging over the back of the chair. I snuck a quick look at Evana. She was running her fingers over Robert's library. I slipped a bug in behind his lapel. Fingers crossed.

"Hey, wanna do a line with me? This party is boring. Robert never pays attention to me. He's always with his cronies, taking shop. I really hate it." The Grecian goddess started pouting. I didn't say anything. "Do you have a man, Sara?"

I coughed; these questions always made me uneasy. "I am happily single." The truth was, I wasn't. Just the cases took up all my time. Nobody had crossed my path that made me want to give them a piece. I went on a few lame dates, and whined to my girlfriends like any other woman.

Evana laughed, "Live a little! Sure you don't wanna go home with someone tonight? It's easily done." She said it in a sing-song-y voice.

"Nah, I'm good." Evana chuckled - which annoyed me. Her high, silky ponytail swayed, and her toothy grin came through. She was truly beautiful. Evana showed me around the bathrooms in the house. More smooth cold marble floors, and golden handles in the washbasins. His and her showers existed in each bathroom, with enormous vanity mirrors in both.

"This isn't Robert's taste you know; he inherited the house from his father. They passed it down to him."

"I see. I was wondering why you had diamonds in the door."

"Crazy, huh?"

"Kinda." I was beginning to not be shocked by all that I saw.

That explained the old-world Liberace vibe. Even the wash basin had Elliot's initials on it. I could sleep in there - it was so big. We entered a separate cinema room with surround sound, and fifty chairs for guests to watch private movies. This was so much better than the movie theatre. *Awesome*. If pressed - I mean - I could do the high life. Just minus all the outlandish parties and fuckery. Fly me around the world, and that will be fine.

I must have looked goofy, and awestruck because Evana picked up the remote. The surround sound started kicking in. She poked her tongue out at me from across the room. A massive fifty-foot screen dropped down from the ceiling, and lit up. A circular bar on the left occupied the back corner of the room to entertain guests. The bar held a full stock of alcohol. This was a house of entertainment. On both walls were classic music records in glass frames. I took a closer look: one was a signed record from Elvis Presley. The other, a signed record by the Rolling Stones. A picture sat underneath with Robert and Mick Jagger in it. I bet they shared a memory or two. I surveyed the room, scouting for clues.

The screen started talking, and a movie played within seconds. The surround sound dropped in and was sensational. It felt like I was part of the movie. Evana turned it off and proceeded with the tour. But - not before pouring a drink at the bar. She handed me another, sparkling with her slender fingers. I accepted. A painting of Marilyn Monroe bathed in light hung on the wall. A classic symbol of beauty and grace. The artist had captured the true essence of her light. I noticed a string hanging out the side of the painting. *Noted.* I touched my breast briefly. Inside the top half of my bra, was a small camera. New technology courtesy of Hawk. I pressed it lightly, and a faint click went off. I coughed to cover it, so Evana couldn't hear. I had just taken a picture of what my intuition told me was access to a safe of some sort. Something sat behind that picture. I wanted to figure out what it was. I added the mental imagery to my list.

Next was the workout room, and basically a small gym. This house had mega-richness written all over it. Yoga mats were in their holsters to the left. Weights were stacked neatly right next to them. Straps for suspension training hung from the ceiling and were in the top right corner. I was shocked to see rings hanging from the ceiling as well. Was this guy a gymnast or something? Robert was becoming more and more exciting by the minute. Evana noticed me staring at the rings.

"Yeh, he loves those rings. Robert used to be a gymnastics fanatic as a kid." *Flexible, and risky.* My mind began to wonder about how flexible he was… and what his hips could do. I shook off the thought. I had been doing a lot of that since I got to the Elliot mansion. Three treadmills were lined up. Side by side. I imagined Elliot's Adonis-like body glistening with sweat beads, as he dried himself off from his workout. Sent my hormones into overdrive. Here I was lusting over a criminal, and it was only day one. A cold shower would be the first order of business when I got home. It was crazy, the feelings I was having.

Maybe Hawk was right…

5

HAWK

♟

Turkey sandwich time for me. My knees creaked as I sat down on my back deck. I was hurting after a hard workout. Felt good though, when the ache set in afterwards. I knew my muscles would repair to be even stronger. I usually hit the gym early and got it outta the way. Now I had real work to do on this case. My mind started pondering. Never a good thing in my mind. Pondering. Not really my style. I wasn't a ponderer. More of a 'doing' man myself. Yet here I was…Thinking about the early days with Evana. The case had done that. Brought all these memories flooding back. *Damn you to hell, Evana.*

Those days were bliss. Until she started to slip away from my grip. I tried to pacify her with the passion of our lovemaking, but she started switching off from me. Turning cold like the icy winter nights of Manhattan with no gloves. We all know that's a bitch to deal with. She partied harder than usual. She kept heading to this one club. I admit I followed her there. I started to get a little obsessive.

That's where I first encountered Mr. Playboy, as Sara nicknamed him. I really despised losing. Especially to billionaire dweebs. I don't know if she switched off from me because I didn't give her enough information. I was an assassin for hire, so eluding questions should have been my forté. She knew something was up with me. She could have been a spy herself. I told her I was an I.T. specialist working with private clients. What a crock. I was far from I.T. unless you counted deciphering codes, numbers and coordinates to trap bad guys. Like Batman, I had a basement operation going on with all my gear and satellites set up. If anyone ever made it down to my lair, they still wouldn't be able to enter.

"You haven't shown me *all* of your apartment, babe."

"What? The man cave? That's a real sight. Spy shit, and all sorts. Nothing you want to see." She waved me off with a light laugh. I gauged the reaction on her face. You see, that's the common trick. For the truth is stranger than fiction. I never lied to her. I told her the truth. Just the thought of someone you're dating being an international spy and assassin seems so outrageous your brain can't comprehend it.

"Ok, ok I get it. The man cave is off-limits." Then we made love. No more mancave talk after that. But she lingered a little too long, peering down the stairs sometimes…Evana had a curious spirit. I wished now more than ever I'd risked it. Who knows where we'd be now? Maybe she would have joined me for the ride. Now, I would never know.

To open the steel trap automatic door, you had to know how to enter. On the wall next to the door, a panel existed. My fingerprints were required to make the dashboard emerge and pop out of the wall. On the panel, a sexy lady, way better than Siri, would ask you for a retina scan, followed by a code. Only then would the steel doors, heavy enough to crush a human, open.

On the top of the iceberg, my place looked like a stock, standard bachelor pad. A nice living room with a big screen. Some of my prized Hawk feathers framed on the wall that my

Grandfather Chief gave me. A decent-size chaise lounge rounded it all out. I'm too tall for those prissy little two-seaters. I didn't have a lot of visitors for obvious reasons, and liked it that way. I had too much at stake. You never knew when you were up against a covert spy.

When Mr. Playboy popped up, I realized the pain of losing someone. Evana's partying and cheating made me feel like a raging red river was running through me. Reminded me of the rivers that ran when I lived on the Virginia reservation with my Grandfather, Black Hawk. He was the great one I was named after. What an honor. One I didn't take lightly. I recalled following Evana to the club she frequented this one night. I hung in the back with my cap low, watching and witnessing this schmaltzy player in action.

I saw the twisting of the tide between me and her. The way Mr. Playboy looked at her like she was a New York breakfast slice. He didn't care for her. He was just some over-sexed stud out to take his lady. *Who was this fuckface?* Cut to the background checks...This dude smelled of bad news. His business dealings on the surface were somewhat clean, and his company was making money hand over fist. His core group was shadier than a mob boss in a casino, according to the records I sourced. A bunch of things weren't adding up for me with this guy. Elliot came from a wealthy, old money family with strong ties to the U.S. Homeland Security network. I was yet to find out how deep those ties were.

He dodged an investigation for the murder of a student. She disappeared on a college campus years ago. I found out he had direct links to her, because she ran the school paper. She'd interviewed him several times regarding the debate team he was on. All the other students were questioned, except him. Every time an incident occurred in, and around him, he went AWOL. Whenever his companies were being investigated, he rose unscathed. The incidents were heard in the news, and never spoken of again. Covered up. Almost as if people were being silenced or paid off. Shit. Just wasn't kosher to me.

I snuck out the back door of the club that night. I knew things were pretty much over for me and Evana. I would ask her where she went. With her sexy, haughty lips, she would taunt me, and profess pretty little lies with a straight face.

"I was just out with the girls…" or "Don't worry about where I was." I had to hold myself back from ambushing Elliot with a roundhouse kick, then finishing him off by stomping on his head.

Somehow, I managed to keep my cool. All the military training helped me to restrain myself. One of the training exercises of my unit was to remain stoic in the face of adversity, even if it involved torture. To not rat out your country if you were captured by the enemy. Too late for me on that front. I followed both the money trail, and my own sense of justice. Hence, the rogue assassin title.

One night, I watched her at the club for about two hours, waiting for her back at the apartment. *This shit had to stop. I swear my blood pressure had risen a thousand notches. I must have had it bad. I'm an assassin, not too much can raise my blood pressure.*

Evana would come home eventually that night. Or should I say five a.m. the next morning. *How could I still love her in those moments?* I don't know, but I did. I started to resent her; that wasn't a good thing. The night of the split with Evana brought a river to the shore. That raging river ended up overflowing. Almost like an out of body experience when I saw her. She stumbled in drunk, failing to realize her nipple was hanging out over her dress. When I moved closer, a number was smudged in red lipstick: "Call Me," it said. My military knots of control frayed, and threatened to snap loose.

"Are you cheating on me, Evana? Is there someone else? Why not just tell me?" My defenses were up. The answer:

clear as day, and black as night. A rhetorical question at that point.

"You can't control me... I will and can do whatever I want. I don't even know you!" That stung, because it was true. Her trash-talking continued.

"That's not what I'm asking you. It's a straightforward question. I mean, you let some clown put red lipstick on your chest." I silently seethed as my words spat out at her.

"Oh yeh, that's nothing." She gestured to her chest, attempting to wipe the remnants of evidence away. "It's from an edgy photoshoot I just finished. Ya know. One of those." Her eyes diverted to her feet in guilt. I lied to her about my double life, and she lied to me about hers. If that wasn't a mirror, I don't know what was.

"Alright, so this is the game we're playing, huh? You're lying to me, and all I'm asking for is the truth."

"I guess we both are." She looked at me with her big luminous eyes. "I ask you about your life, and your friends. You never seem to want to let me in. So, at the end of the day..." Her voice trailed off. "I will do what I want." She gazed through me like glass. I let out a heavy sigh. No come back for that one. I wouldn't risk my cover. I knew this crossroad would come as it did every time. I was better off dating a government official, I swear.

"See? You can't answer me, either. I know you're not an I.T. specialist that's for sure." I looked at her for a long time. A moment existed where I thought to spill the beans, but I resisted. My mouth remained wired shut.

"Well if you can't trust me, then it's best I leave." *Safe route. Ending on an amicable note.*

"Yeh, I guess so." Her mouth twitched, she wanted to cry. The champagne high from the club outing was over. The Grim Reaper of relationships had come to the door to cut the cords.

She started crying, tears falling from her pretty face. I

reached for her to say sorry for how it was ending. She started speaking with an eerie quietness. Her voice whittled down to a tiny whisper. "You need to leave. Take your clothes and just go." Her eyes were glassy. I tried to reason. I knew she wouldn't listen – it would have come out like I was begging her, anyway.

If a bow and arrow were the weapon of choice, one just shot into my heart that night. I grabbed my shit, and packed like an army soldier. Evana was slumped at the marble glass tabletop in the open plan kitchen. She had a cigarette hanging out of her lips. Shaky slender fingers were grasping it. Her red crimson lipstick smeared on her cheek. Midnight black mascara settled into the grooves of her face. Her pupils were heavily dilated. I faced her one last time.

"I love you." Chords of despair bubbled up in me, hoping it might be enough to smooth us over. For the first time in a long time, I wanted to stay with this woman.

She waved me off. "Don't. It's over Hawk – you have to accept it. We had a good run. It's been a bunch of fun, and all that."

"So that's it? You're just going to spit me out, just like that?" I fumed. "Who is it, Evana?"

Silence.

"Someone who knows how to have a good time." There. She admitted it. The truth shall set you free. In this case, it really didn't make me feel better. Just hollow. I walked out the door and left Evana smoking her cigarette. I drove into the dark that night with a midnight soul. I would come good. Like I always did when it ended. This one stung a little too long for my liking. *Crucifixion*.

Now I had a bone to pick with Robert, the Playboy. For stealing my girl, and to bring home my paycheck. *The new mark*. The more I probed into Elliot, the more I found out this guy was off. A few years back a successful shipping magnate, who owned one of the major shipping operations at the Port of New York docks, was found dead. Cluster Ferman. Shot execution style and slumped precariously behind one of the shipping containers. The authorities called it suicide. And would you look-a here, none other than Elliot Enterprises sprung up a few months later. With what? Full ownership rights of the docks. Not a rinky-dink coincidence. This dude was a cunning criminal who needed to be stopped in his tracks.

Lo and behold my little protégé, Sara, mentions she needs help on a case.

"Hey, I got this case with a supermodel involved. Think you can help?"

"What's the names? Evana... I can't remember her name right off top, the other is Robert Elliot." My blood almost froze over the day she told me. My past, bringing unfinished business to my doorstep. I decided not to reveal my relationship with Evana to Sara. I had no intention to complicate matters. Least I could do was get that fucker Elliot off the streets. Plus, I wanted to hear that Evana was doing well in life. I still felt protective of her. I jumped at the chance to get in on the case.

"Sure I can help out. Send me the details and I'll see what I can find out."

Her case piggybacked off a much bigger investigation. One that my government connect had running. I made up my mind I would feed Sara breadcrumbs, and she could work out the rest. Keep her out of harm's way. Mr. Playboy was in deep pockets of hurt, negotiating with drug cartel lords from a foreign country. Yes, I had the inside scoop. This was the sole reason I was assigned. The dude was out of his depth on this one.

Those guys didn't fuck around. They sliced and diced fingers like child's play. I'm talking about the Columbians. They were coming to North America to spread their wings, and their operation. They fancied themselves in the game of intelligence. X-ray intelligence, and black-market cyber stuff. My government official clients didn't take too kindly to this. "Hawk, we give you a license to shoot to kill."

"Got it."

"If you get caught, we can't protect you. It's blood on your hands not ours." Hence, why I needed to be anonymous. Hawk wasn't my government name. Nobody knew that. Not even Sara. The prototype my superior was searching for had been declared missing two weeks ago from a secret government unit. My guess was an international leak, a loose link inside government headquarters. They didn't give me that intel. Just retrieve the data, plain and simple. If the prototype wound up in the wrong hands it would be sold to the highest bidder on the black market. Millions of dollars, possibly billions, and the ultimate takedown of nations across the globe. These were the stakes. I was in two minds if I wanted Evana back. What I was certain about was Elliot being locked up for a long time. If he needed to be taken out so be it…

6

SARA

♟

Back to the par-tay. Robert leaned in the doorway frame as we came around the corner from his office. *Had he followed us up here to keep an eye?* He threw us a curious look. "Well, what do we have here?"

Evana wobbled, gesturing with her right hand in a weird way. "Just giving Sara the grand tour." She came across as nervous, might be the drugs in her system, but still... *Mental note.*

Robert's mouth grinned at me, but his blue eyes held suspicion. "I see." Behind those words I read a warning sign.

"And what did you think?" Elliot shuffled a few things around his desk in passive anger. He wasn't happy that we were in his office. I saw his beautiful jawline set. The palpable tension floated around the room. I grabbed my neck, and kneaded out the tension. Something about this guy truly left me unbalanced. Like a flashing neon 70's sign-in fluoro pink. *Danger, danger run for your life!* At the same time, I felt a strange sensation of excitement snaking around the pit of my stomach.

"You seem to really like your mahogany." I cleared my throat hesitantly as he smirked in his response.

"Yeah, that's what happens when you're from the old money world. You inherit into greatness. Big shoes to fill, but I think I manage pretty well," he said calmly. Letting me know who's boss. *You might have money, but you don't have sense.* I gave him the once-over.

"Robert, darling, where were you headed?" Evana changed the subject.

"I'm here to collect some documents," he answered tightly.

"You're not working during the party, are you? You're a party pooper scooper." She held up a long finger towards him, touching his nose. Seemed like a gesture to subdue Robert. Robert frowned momentarily as if irked by Evana's statement.

"I thought you came from old money?" I threw in my two cents.

"Touché. Still, I have to maintain the legacy, right? Besides, my guests are thoroughly entertained – that's for sure. They don't need me for that. I've got a deal to close. Now is the time to get the papers signed. While they're all shitfaced. Parker has been sitting on this deal for months. Who knew all it took was a couple of chicks to keep him happy?" He added arrogantly. I hid my shock at his gall. *More reveals.* I didn't expect Robert to be so open about his business dealings. Or maybe he wasn't saying anything at all...

Would the mic pick up this conversation? I would soon find out how good Hawk's spyware was. The information Elliot carelessly released might prove useful to building a case around. Not that I could use it. But it might be enough to find some other minor legal angle. *Keep him talking, Sara.*

"I guess so. Is this where you do a lot of your business, or do you have a downtown office?" I knew the answer, but I wanted to see how he would respond.

"You're asking a lot of questions tonight, Ms. Sara. An inquisitive one, huh?" He toyed with the paperweight on the desk.

"Just interested. Wondering." I shrugged my shoulders, like it was no big deal. My heart sped up when I saw him pick up the paperweight. *Put it down. Put it down. Please.*

"I split my time between here and LA. I have clients in Hollywood. Some of them are downstairs at the party. You might have noticed. I own a penthouse downtown, too." His eyes penetrated mine. I held his intrusive gaze this time. I wasn't backing down.

"You seem to live an interesting life," I quipped as I moistened my lips in nervousness.

"You don't know the half of it. I'm sure I will be seeing more of you, since you're working so closely with Evana." The hidden invite right under his wife's nose. Cool heads prevail, so they say – and that's just how I kept it. Evana watched on with translucent eyes, sipping her champagne. Numbness circulated through them.

I pushed the envelope with Elliot a little further. "Surely, you're not signing a contract tonight?" I mirrored Evana's sentiments.

"Oh, so innocent, Ms. Vogue? Surely you know how to mix business with pleasure, no?" His eyes darkened. There he went again, undressing me with his wintry baby blues. I was shirking under duress. *Mayday mayday...* That cocky smile lifted the corners of his mouth up again at my jitters. I stood awkwardly in the middle of the conversation. I shifted my gaze to Evana; she caught onto Robert's flirt game. He suddenly grabbed her tiny waist and planted a saucy tongue kiss on her. In front of me. The creepiest thing about it, was Elliot looked straight at me when he did it.

"Won't be long, babe. Show your li'l friend, Sara, the kick-ass fountain that's out back."

"Good idea." Evana replied meekly. Elliot had tranquilized her.

"I will see you ladies in a bit. Duty calls." Robert shot her a brazen smile as he entered the heavy mahogany doors of his office and shut them behind him.

Evana whispered, "Ok let's go. Robert doesn't like anyone snooping around in his office."

At least I would have surveillance to play back from tonight. I could chop it up with Hawk tomorrow for a breakdown. Meanwhile, I planned to do everything I could to tease more intel from Evana. Back through the circus, down the stairs to the back patio. More moaning reverberating from rooms down the hall.

"What is going on down there?" I hissed to Evana. She lifted her heavily arched eyebrows at me.

"What's going on? Something you couldn't handle." She put a finger underneath my chin, and giggled. I had an inkling, and that just cemented it.

Evana opened the magnificent glass doors. They gave way to a view of a supersize pool. Smack bang in the middle of it was a fountain. Lives of the rich and famous. He said a fountain, but in the middle of the pool? *You have got to be kidding me.* Only the Elliot's. The fountain had lighting streaming through it which switched to different rhythms when the colors changed. Wading pools were on either side of the fountain, and blocked off into square sections. A very elaborate Miami-style get up. Small huts of shelter surrounded the pool with umbrellas, ready to be opened for frolicking in the sun. All you needed was a Cabana boy to bring you cocktails, and the dream would be complete. Who needed to go to Cabo if you had this?

I watched Evana sit on the water's edge. She hitched her Grecian-style dress, and jumped into the pool. "Glad you don't mind about your dress," I sang out sarcastically.

Evana let out a drunken laugh. "This old thing? Don't you

like to get a little wild, Sara? I've got plenty of 'em. Plus, designers give me shit all the time. And why wouldn't they?" Even in her drunken stupor, her goddess features were evident. Stunning. The strobe lights from the fountain hit the golden highlights in her hair just right. It reminded me of the legend about the lady emerging from the Trevi fountain.

"I'll skip the pool tonight. Plus, Maurice wants his dress back."

"Ha! Let me tell you how many dresses have gone missing since I started working at that office." Evana started counting on her fingers, and holding them up. This supermodel was also a superbrat. *What the hell?*

"Oh no, not all mine honey. Other Vogue assistants. What do you think they work there for? The clothes, and to flex to their friends. You'll learn." *Oh no I won't. I plan to get this case solved, and get on with my life.*

Without warning, an odd sensation of heat overcame me. Forcing me to peer up. Sure enough Mr. Playboy had his heavy-duty velvet curtains pulled back. He was watching from the upstairs window. His gaze held a dark heaviness. A weird sensation fluttered in my stomach. *Did he suspect?* Was he wondering why we were in his office? I didn't know whether to throw him a wave, or to ignore him. He wasn't smiling. His overbearing stare began to bother me. Evana captured where my eyeline was taking me.

"He's watching, isn't he?" She heaved herself out of the pool. "Come on, let's go back to the party." Her gown was heavy from the weight of the water. Her dress clung to her, like one of those girls from a wet T-shirt contest. My presence was done for the night. If I stayed any longer, shit would go down. Time to go.

"Actually Evana, I'm going to head out. I have a meeting with Maurice at the office tomorrow," I lied.

"Are you still doing induction? I thought you were done with that?"

"Well, there's a few things that Maurice has to cover with me. It's going to be early." I faked a yawn as we made our way back to the house.

Evana's face was one of discontent. "I can't relate to any of Robert's people. None of them take me seriously. They're always talking shit, and speaking in code."

My ears perked up like a bloodhound on a trail who had just found the scent. "How do you know he's speaking in code, Evana?"

"Oh, it's just horseshit." She lit up another cigarette in her slender fingers. "Some shit about round two at the Apollo is going down tomorrow. You know some spy-sounding crap. He thinks I'm too spaced out to know. But I do. I remember one time I came home from partying. He thought I was too drunk to notice. His cronies were lifting a garbage bag in the trunk. I only had a couple of drinks that night. I pretended I was high, so I wouldn't get busted."

First thought that came into my mind… *Was it Michael?*

"Uh-huh." I kept my voice on an even keel. I wanted her to keep on blabbering. We were approaching the house. I knew she would clam up once we got there, so I slowed our pace down.

"Pretty heavy accusation. Did you ever see Robert have anything to do with the bags? What do you think was in the bags?" I went for the jugular.

"Bodies." She let out a weird fake laugh. "Maybe, who knows?" She shrugged her shoulders nonchalantly, doubling back on what she said. "I could see the outline. He's too smart to touch the bags. He doesn't like getting his hands dirty, maybe he has guys for that. Plus, I don't like cops. Robert has half of them pissing in his pocket anyway. He's like fucking royalty or something. Nobody can touch him in New York. One day he is going to get busted big time." Evana shook her head several times, like she didn't believe what she was saying herself.

"Sounds crazy to me. Ever thought of calling the anonymous tip line, and letting the authorities handle it?" *Keep her talking, Sara. Just keep her talking.*

"As long as he keeps buying me bags, darling!" She mimicked in an English voice.

"Why did you marry Robert, Evana?" My curious mind wanted to know.

"Well he's hot, rich, and has all the good drugs. Plus, he's killer in the sack. What more could I want? He's pretty good like that. I have gotten a lot of model gigs, because I'm with him. It's like a business partnership with benefits, really. I look good on his arm."

We were at the house. *Food for thought.* Evana had no idea who she was messing with. If she knew the full spectrum of the guy, she might not be with him. But, then again if you saw dead bodies go into trunks - chances are, you probably knew. I needed to go home. I wanted to see if I could pick up any transmissions between Robert, and his fellow alleged felons. Anything that might give me an inch…

"Evana, thank you for inviting me to the party. I gotta go now. I guess I'll see you at the photo shoot, tomorrow afternoon?"

"Yuh, you will. I will be looking fab and glam as always!" She giggled throwing her head back. She resembled a bedraggled rat at this point. Not so glam. She retrieved my phone from the mystery dip bowl. I made my way to the ultra-expensive door. Not without a few men vying for my attention on the way out. Hot lava felt like it was being poured down my back. *Robert.* He was following me to the door from the staircase.

"Let me grab your coat for you," he said smoothly.

"Uh ok, I was just going to grab it myself…"

"Well, what kind of man would let a lady grab her own coat?" He threw me a silky smile that made my knees go weak. *Gather yourself, Sara.* An attraction is *not* happening. I repeat this is *not* happening. You do not feel *anything* for this guy. He is a killer. A playboy. Stop thinking of him without clothes on. Stop thinking of stroking your fingers down his lean torso. Luckily, he wasn't a mind reader as well as a murderer. That would be a case to tell a story about.

"Thank you, Robert, and nice to meet me- I mean meet you." My words got mixed up. *Damn.* Gotta go. Right. *Now.*

"The pleasure, was definitely all mine." He grabbed my hand, the nerve endings in my fingers sent a rippling shock-wave through me. He lifted it to his lips, and kissed it. Robert's full lips on top of my hand. I struggled to restrain myself. I yanked my hand back as a precautionary measure.

"I hope to see you soon, Sara." He flashed a devious smile.

"I'm sure I will see you around. I'll be at a photo shoot with Evana tomorrow." I wanted him to remember that he was very much married, and that I was not up for grabs. I think I desperately wanted to convince myself as well.

"Ah, yes – my lovely wife." Almost, as if he forgot she existed. "She's amusing our guests – that's for sure." Knots in my stomach had me inching closer to the front door.

"Ok, I have a big day tomorrow. Thanks, and bye bye." I ignored his comments about Evana.

I practically ran out of the door before he could say anything else. I sucked in a deep breath. I made it out of the circus alive. The man almost lulled me into his arms. His powers of seduction were overwhelming. *I mean, what was I thinking?* Maybe it was because I had been working so hard. I had forgotten my mind, and left it somewhere in the depths of the ocean. The deep blue sea. Home time, and away to wash off Robert's spell.

Home sweet home. I made fast work of the freeway. Before I knew it, I had parked my wedges, and slid some chips in the oven. I was starving. No good snacks at the party unless you liked drugs. I poured myself a red wine for good measure. I didn't drink that much. I spaced my drinks out throughout the night. I wanted to stay sharp to see the situation clearly. I drank enough to be sociable, and not suspicious... I changed wearily into my PJ's and went straight to my recorder to play-back Elliot's phone transcriptions.

The tape clicked in as I listened intently with my glass of red sitting beside me. Robert's slanderous voice hit the airwaves...

"Slick Rick is ready to roll. I just need to get the big boys to play. The spot is up in the air... Secure it by June 15."

June 15 was only a few weeks away. Something was going down. Slick Rick? What kinda code was that? Was that a drug shipment?

I kept listening; *Told you, Clope, that's not how it's going to roll. We make a move on my go ahead. Slick Rick will put you in instant retirement, my friend. It's a wrap. You ain't gotta worry no more. Just hang in there. Things are a little hot right now, so let's cool our jets. You know, since that little incident."*

Incident? What incident? Clope? Sounded like one of Robert's goons. *Instant retirement?* Where and what time was the big question. They said June 15, but time wasn't mentioned. If I could tip off the feds in time... I could lead them right to the bust. I had to report back to my client in a few days for an update. Relief washed over me. I had a lead at least. Maybe it would trigger something in the client's memory from his dealings with Robert.

"Alright, Clope. You just keep the guys in position, and I will see you Friday. I gotta run, I got some hotties waiting for me." Robert's throaty laugh came through the wire. Even his laugh reminded me of butter.

7

SARA

♟

A hazy sun rose over Maywood as I got ready to meet Evana for the afternoon photoshoot. My first one! I felt excited to be trying something totally new. I grabbed a coffee from my local haunt on the way to the shoot. I arrived on site fifteen minutes early. A plethora of props were strewn everywhere. Racks of designer clothes were lined up off to the left-hand side of the street. We were on location in a well-known spot. The meatpacking district of New York. It was known as a trendy and hip area to frequent. A place for the glamour pusses and cool young kids. It got its name from the 1900's where it once housed slaughterhouses and packing plants. In the '80's, the region graduated to the sector known for drug trafficking and overall seedy behavior. The meatpacking district had come a long way since then.

I had no frickin' idea what my role would be at the shoot, but I decided to roll with it. *Me!* Working at Vogue. Who knew? Wait 'till I bragged to my gal pals.

I was on the Vogue set. Yeh. That's right. Vogue.
Shut your mouth!

I chuckled a little to myself about it. I had a few tight-knit friends from childhood that remained dear to me the whole way through my life. I knew I could depend on them, and they could depend on me. Lately, not so much because of my caseload; but overall, I was loyal to them. They would no doubt laugh and roll their eyes at my colorful, oddball life. Maurice cooperated, saying it was ok for me to be on set.

"We could use an extra assistant. You could come in handy after all. Just don't mess up." I was to be given simple jobs. It wouldn't be a dead giveaway. I remembered Maurice rolling his eyes the first day I showed up to the Vogue headquarters. He had looked me up and down, and clutched his chest in mock horror.

"Yikes, we gotta get you out of those nylon stockings honey. They are doing nothing for those pins." He explained that I would be 'Vogue-a-fied,' as he called it.

On today's shoot, I was to assist an elegant Japanese art director named Yoshimoto. Super stylish man. He wore a black jacket with matching velour at the bottom of the sleeves, a red linen shirt, and white loafers. A high jet-black man bun sat on top of his head. The more sophisticated version of Jet Li. He gave me the job of safety pinning, providing nipple covers and bits and pieces for the girls on shoot, including Evana. It was what they called an 'editorial shoot,' the vibe to be emulated was 'artsy.'

Part of Gansevoort Street had been blocked off with barricades to accommodate the shoot. Five stunning models were present on location. I hoped for a prick free experience. *From the safety pins, of course.* What if my hand slipped? What a nightmare. I mean, hasn't the safety pin dress been done to death? Didn't Liz Hurley do that already?

Evana looked every part the supermodel with her dewy and demure makeup. A white sheet draped her body beautifully along with a pair of fire-red heels. My job was to safety pin the sides for a funky edge. To show off the shoes. That's what the client wanted. Each model wore different shoes with the same white sheet. The photographer wanted to capture the models in a jumping pose. Quite clever, really.

Two hours into the shoot, devoid of any prickly connections, I was just about to head over to Evana and pin her when Elliot slid onto the scene. *This guy again.* We were in the middle of a photo shoot. The models started gawking at him and whispering. Giggling like gaggles of geese. Possibly, the black Maserati he rolled up in made their necks snap his way. Money has its own language regardless of who was behind it.

Elliot's look – since we're talking fashion – saw him in a navy-blue suit jacket, crisp light blue shirt, and Italian loafers. Every inch the likeness of a stereotypical rich playboy with a hot blonde wife. I wanted to grab some popcorn and take a seat. This scene had all the elements of turning into a show. How the hell was Yoshimoto going to feel about this intervention at his carefully-curated Vogue shoot? Meanwhile, I was tending to all the haberdashery requirements for the models, sewing up little arm holes in their sheets.

Yoshimoto turned to Robert and gave him one of those macho hand-grippy things. He gave him a slap on the back like old pals. Not long after, he signaled for the models to take five. *So, they knew each other and were willing to stop the shoot for Robert.* My mouth hung agape with disbelief. Robert swung a smile my way, dropping his sunglasses with a wink. I just stood there as if in a time lapse.

A fleeting rush of unwanted heat flowed to my cheeks. I wanted to override these biological impulses threatening to derail my entire system. If feelings were a lightbulb, I would want them turned off now. Eventually after a little chit chat with Yoshimoto, Elliot made it over to me.

"Hi, Sara – nice to see you. Hope you're not working too hard." Silk singing to my ears. Next came the undressing. I felt intensely vulnerable in my denim cutoffs. He ran his eyes over my legs for way too long. At least I shaved and wore one of my favorite striped tees. *Wait a minute. Didn't they say hori-zontal stripes make you look fat? Urgh. If I had had time to run home and change, I would have.*

"Well, now you're here, I could use a break. It's pretty hot out here today." I didn't like the way that escaped my mouth. I wasn't trying to be seductive.

"Yeh, it is. You look especially hot," Robert hit back with a warm chuckle. My cheeks started to flush again; my face was letting me down. It was annoying the effect this man had on me.

"Umm... yeah, it's warm. I need a drink." Robert walked off to grab a mineral water from the model's station. *Why was Robert here? What would make him stop a photo shoot in the Meat-packing District in the middle of the day?*

A short time later, Elliot came back, handing me a sparkling mineral water. His hand lightly brushed mine. Lightning ran through my wrist, jarring my tender senses. He felt it, too. His cool blue eyes grew soft when we touched. *Feelings rising from a killer?* No. Couldn't be. Conflicting thoughts sifted through my brain. I wanted him to leave, but I also wanted him to stay so I could find out his next move.

"So, what brings you downtown? This is pretty far from your office." Breezily curious is how I wanted to appear. I'm pretty sure I failed.

"Yoshimoto is an old friend of mine; he asked me to stop by. And to check on my lovely wife and her new friend." Robert shined his pearlies at me. I noted that he said 'checked,' not 'see.' *Oh, Robert – how I see you.* I cannot be fooled. But I let the game run its course with a fake smile that didn't reach my eyes.

"Must be a pretty good friend if you're willing to come down here in the middle of a photo shoot," I mumbled.

"Slow day at the office. I can afford to spend some time." He looked off into the distance as he gulped down his water. I watched his sexy lips wrap around the bottle, wishing it was my lips instead. I blinked rapidly to move the impish thought from my mind.

"I see. Nice to see your wife doing her model thing on location. I'm sure she'll be happy to see you." *Not.*

"Well, I'm not so certain about that. But I know this. Any friend of my wife's is a friend of mine." Robert resumed ogling my legs with no shame. *Really? More like keep your enemies close, but I digress.*

Yoshimoto signaled to Robert. Great, I was off the hook. Robert turned his head slightly on the walk-off.

"I look forward to connecting with you again soon, Sara."

"See you later, Robert." The hairs on the back of my neck were standing up. Undercurrents of serious desire threatened to jeopardize this case if my emotional cup ran over.

Still couldn't work out why he was here. What business did Mr. Playboy and Yoshimoto have together? My suspicions were soon confirmed. I saw them walk into a nearby warehouse entry and head upstairs. As they walked to the staircase, I caught a peek of Robert slipping a small bag to Yoshimoto in a smooth handshake motion. The drug shake. Evana came up behind Robert to bear hug him. This guy brought drugs directly to the photo shoot? Didn't he have runners for that? Mighty strange to me. All three of them moved slightly out of sight up the stairs. Great news is I planted a listening device behind the tag of Robert's blazer. A small square that resembled a piece of clear Scotch tape. Blink and you'd miss it. The navy blue one he left in the office at the party. *Ingenious, huh?* I got it from my main man, Hawk. I had my doubts at the time when I pinned the device on the jacket. There were no guarantees Robert would even wear that particular jacket. But, today was my lucky day. His broad shoulders were fitting snugly into the jacket. Navy blue pinstripes and all. *Oh yeah, baby.*

The other models looked unbothered by the interruption. Seemed almost commonplace. Twenty minutes passed by and they'd planted themselves on the curb, sipping their bottles of water. The New York sun was beating down on their backs and mine. They were waiting for the shoot to resume. The unbothered looks faded soon enough. They were replaced with agitation. No models wanted to be wrapped up in a white silk sheet on a hot summer's day. I'm sure all their feet were swelling from the heat. Five minutes passed before Yoshimoto and Evana resurfaced, and we got back to work. Yoshimoto emerged with remnants of white powder under his left nostril. If you weren't looking too hard, everything seemed fine. But my highly trained eye caught the thin ring around his nose. He was snorting drugs on location. This shit was an epidemic. All I knew was, if you couldn't function and had to stop a shoot to snort, you were addicted.

Yoshimoto came back to the middle of the street, clapping the palms of his hands together. Much like he had clag glue stuck to them and was trying to pull it apart. "Ok girls, we are back to work! Let's do this." I spotted Robert slinking away in the background. I watched with interest as his black Maserati drove off. The photographer got the models back in motion with action shots. Fascinating what scenes Yoshimoto could create, despite his vices. Seemed like it helped him be more creative. More dynamic. I watched him work and review the shots then and there. The shoot drew a small crowd of onlookers and wolf whistlers from the basketball court right near it. The models paid no attention to them. I stood back and admired my handiwork. Not too bad for a first-time assistant. All in all, the shoot was a hit, and Evana worked the camera like a pro.

From this shoot, I learned modeling required a lot of stamina and standing around. I was beginning to appreciate the fashion world a little more. There must have been over a three hundred photos taken, all with some sort of re-adjustment from the models. Who knows how many of them would be used.

For some reason, the energy between me and Evana shifted…I don't know when and how it happened, but it did. Like a thorn in my side maybe. I felt like I existed between a rock and a hard place. I couldn't shake this attraction to Robert. Maybe my soul held a deeper dark side after all. In a way, I fought against wanting to befriend Evana. That was *her* husband and I was trying to nail him to the wall. *How could I like this guy?* My main goal in life involved fighting for justice for my clients. Giving them hope. Shining a light into the dark corners so they could heal and move on. Sometimes, the delicate balance of how far to take situations came up. A moral dilemma clause that had to be exercised with care. My track record spoke for itself. I usually wavered on illegal versus legal methods. Sometimes rules are meant to be broken or manipulated every now and then. Right now, my moral compass tinkered on the edge of resolute danger fantasizing about a smooth crime boss with evil intent.

I was on my third sparkling water and felt like I was roasting. The sizzling New York sun and Elliot's presence had me burning.

Evana made her way over to me after the shoot was said and done. "Hey, you."

"Hey yourself," I replied. "So, you guys were on break for a while. Does hubby always show up on your shoots?" Evana took in a long drag of a newly lit cigarette, sucking in her incredible cheekbones for maximum nicotine benefits.

"Sometimes. He has some business with Yoshimoto, so I guess he asked him to come down."

"Right." She knew what the hell was up. I saw it right in front of my face, in plain sight.

"I think a lot of the time he's spying on me." Now we're getting somewhere.

"You think he doesn't trust you or something?" I walked and talked with Evana as we approached the clothes rack. I started re-arranging things, preparing to pack down.

"Who knows? But I married him, so God only knows what the problem is," Evana sighed heavily."Hey, you wanna come around for a pool party tonight?' Evana swiftly moved to another subject.

Great. Another opportunity to enter Mr. Playboy's lair. I wondered if my happiness stemmed from another opportunity to crack the case or a longing to see Elliot. The guy was completely off limits, *repeat it again*. The guy is a suspected murderer and serial womanizer. Not to mention involved with a waif-like model who I had a growing protection over. I would have to let this one play out.

What does one wear to a pool party? One where you know the husband of your new acquaintance is potentially the killer of your client?

I settled on a classic black vintage one-piece bathing suit. Halter neck style, with polka dots. I added a sarong with a fringe for extra flair. My attempt at being low key. With a tiny wink of class and pizzazz. *I'll admit it*. The fringe was for me. Maurice introduced me to a thing or two about accentuating my body shape. At the pool party I decided to try my newfound confidence on for size. I rolled up to the Elliot's mansion prepared for what the night would bring. I knew the drill, and that my phone would be snatched. I had other methods of recording. My own wire sat underneath my clothing. I was patched in. The same wiring, I snuck inside Elliot's jacket tag. Hard to detect.

I gave the Elliot's their due credit. Robert sure knew how to flaunt his wealth. The fountain of Trevi was in sight as I entered from the back-side gate, the entrance to the elaborate poolside. Two bodyguards checked me at the door. As predicted, my phone was taken. I heard the music thumping, like last time. The offender being a hyped-up deejay, mixing and scrambling the decks with house music. His booth holding court under a shaded area right by the pool. The night sky formed a coral and cobalt blue blanket across the

New York sky. Elliot had plenty of light cascading over the pool so people could see. I browsed the pool scene to check out any new players.

Women were swimming and cavorting in the pool, some were levitating on large blow up flamingos bobbing around in the chlorinated water. Close your eyes and Miami was right here in New York. The pool consisted of tanned blonde chicks with large hoo-hahs and small triangle bikinis to cover them. They were sipping their cocktails through stripe-y straws and large botoxed lips. Latin women, Black women, Asian women, and all in between were in the water as well. Guys were waxed and bare-chested, lounging around. Some others were doing dive bombs in the pool, making the women recoil from them with disgust. They didn't want their hair getting messed up. Others were dancing on the makeshift dance floor, having fun and goofing around. Generally, a tamer affair than the last party. Felt like a crowd from L.A. and Miami, not New York. Maybe, that's exactly the crowd Robert wanted here.

Speaking of Elliot, he was holed up towards the back of the poolside, leaning across a cream outdoor chair. His lips were moving intently, locked in dialogue with a mafia-looking dude. This guy came straight out of a *Godfather* scene. Surely. Scary stuff. A large gold chain sat around his neck. He was sitting beside a stunning Brazilian woman with legs for days and more white teeth. She was elegantly dressed in a black and gold triangle two-piece swimsuit with a long wrap. *Where was Evana? Why did she invite me if she wasn't going to be here?*

I didn't want to look like a wallflower without anything in my hand. Looked like a pina colada would warm up the proceedings. That way I wouldn't feel so out of place. One of the perks of the job, I would say. Clinking glasses with criminals. I felt Elliot's energy looming; he made eye contact from afar. Uncanny how I knew his eyes were on me. Invisible pieces of string linked us together. He excused himself from his beach chair talk, meandering in my direction. Robert never really walked – he glided. Cream Chinos, open shirt, and a simple chain with a cross on it. *A cross? No. It would take more than a cross to forsake his sins.* His baby blue eyes sunk into me like hot butter soaking into toast. Or was that me melting?

"Hi, Beautiful. Glad you could make it. Evana told me you would be coming to join us this evening – much to my delight." I squared my jaw to him, letting him know I wasn't afraid of him. I sensed his gratification; he didn't take me seriously.

"Thanks for the invite. It looks like you have a private party over there in your corner." I nodded my head in the direction of the Mafia-looking dude. I wanted in. I wanted to know more about the Mafia dude. I sensed he held a lot of Robert's secrets.

"Of course. There's always a private party, Sara," he said evenly. "Care to join us? I will introduce you to my people." He walked slightly ahead of me, leading the way. I looked around the party: no negative energy, just people having fun. Much better than the other circus party he hosted.

"Ok." Two could play this game. I had some work to do before my sense of detachment on this case would be effective. My stomach wouldn't play ball, either, and contained some sort of strange knot that needed soothing. My imp imposter popped up, wanting to play.

"Where is your wife?" I said 'wife' for emphasis, so he wouldn't get any slimy ideas.

"You miss her, huh? Don't worry – I'm sure I can keep you occupied until she arrives. She's wrapping up a photoshoot. She told me to look after you until she gets here. I won't bite... *much.*" He flashed his teeth at me. The whitest teeth I had ever seen in the history of teeth. I'm sure he got them done. *Must ask about his dentistry arrangements.* Right after I make a citizen's arrest for the murder of Michael Sawyer. I inhaled his woody scent... it was divine. I caught myself inhaling just a little too long, the combined scent including his body heat making a mix to die for.

"It's new. Tom Ford. Like it?" My eyes rose to meet Robert's. I must have been way too obvious. My heart started pounding, as I tried to keep a neutral face. *How did he know I was intoxicated by his scent? How could he possibly know that?* This can't be happening. I gathered myself momentarily.

"I'm sorry, what do you mean?" I feigned innocence.

"You sniffed, so I figured it must be my cologne you were smelling. Like the scent? Want me to come closer?" He grinned and poked out his tongue. He threw me off guard with his humor. A giggle escaped; I couldn't help it.

"I think you're close enough, Robert," I pushed back.

Robert's eyes turned into a slant. A sly grin lit up his face.

"Not as close as I would like to be, Sara. I can't help myself," he whispered hoarsely.

"I'm sure your wife wouldn't approve of that..." I answered quietly.

"My wife is a nuisance, and she is not as loyal as you might imagine." Robert side-eyed me with wolfish lust.

"I'm sorry to hear that. I do work for her, so this conversation can't go any further," I said firmly. Hard to balance the scales deftly with this guy. He didn't take no for an answer.

"Sara, it's just a matter of time... I always get the things I want." I raised my eyebrows. If any other guy said that to me, I would have walked away. But he had a hold on me. "You look ravishing, by the way." Those cool baby blues surveyed me with pleasure.

"And what happens when you don't get what you want?" I asked as I licked my lips.

He looked at me closely. "I've never experienced that so I wouldn't know." A reluctant smile crept across his handsome face. "C'mon over, and I will introduce you to everyone. The gang's all here." Scrutinizing eyes were upon us as we approached the lineup of cream outdoor chairs underneath the large umbrella.

"Clope, I would like to introduce you to Sara. Vogue's latest rising star. She works with my beautiful wife, Evana."

Now we're talking. Clope from the tapes. Luckily, Hawk still had links to the police department because officially as a P.I. in NYC wiretaps weren't permitted without permission of one of the alleged persons. Which made no sense. Why would you tell the perp you wanted to tape them? This is where I bent the law a little bit. I would leak the tapes if I had to.

A raspy Boston accent got my attention.

"Hey, li'l lady, looking gorgeous. Just the right fit for Vogue; understated class. I like that." Clope nodded his huge square head with approval. *Was it a Boston accent or a Jersey one I was hearing?* Hard to be sure. I recognized his voice to be the same guy on the other end of the line when I tapped Robert's office. Another piece of the jigsaw puzzle starting to slot together. He stretched out his large, meaty hand. Like him. He had rough calluses, minor cuts and scrapes on them. He reminded me of a pitbull that had gone a few rounds. *Yup, this guy was surely the cleaner-upper.* I didn't want to shake his hand and be infected by his killer energy. Smart me had peach sanitizer in my bag. Yuck. I could jump to logical conclusions here and say he was a large part of Elliot's covert plans. I needed more to go on, though. Where was the link to Sawyer's death? What was Sawyer uncovering that got him chopped up? As far as I knew, software development had no correlation with a drug ring. Was he helping him with an embezzling scheme? I had to peel back the layers to understand more of Elliot's system.

The thrill of investigation is what I lived for. Clope's girlfriend of the moment, I guessed, gave me the once over. Her face clearly said she didn't think of me as the 'understated glamour' type. More like gum on her shoe. I could care less.

My job pertained to solving a murder, not appeasing the crim's woman of the hour.

Raspy Boston said, "And this, Sara, is my wife, Camilla. My second wife! Let's hope she's a keeper." A deep throated raspy chuckle came from Clope's mouth, almost like he was wheezing for air. Robert laughed.

Miss Brazil batted her eyelashes, and crooned, "The only *onnneee* Papi," kissing him on his pock-marked cheek.

Clope lapped it up. "Go get us a drink, would ya?" He slapped her behind as she flounced with her mile-long legs to the drinks table near the deejay booth. Ugh. Male chauvinism at its primal best. *Had to be the money, right?* What some women would do to secure money was beyond me. This age-old story had been going on for centuries. If a man has money, many things can be overlooked or conveniently forgotten. Robert looked me over once more and strategically seated me next to him.

"So, Sara. How's Vogue life treating you? You looked to be in your element the other day when I saw you. What are you wanting to achieve from the position?"

"I-I don't know yet." I wasn't prepared for career questions and stuttered over my words.

"You look like a good personal assistant. I'm looking to fire mine."

Clope laughed and slapped Robert on the knee. "Haha. Not up to scratch, huh, Rob? I know what you mean." The pitbull leered and leaned forward in my direction. I moved my legs away from him in case he thought that we were friendly enough for a knee slap. In my mind, I visualized a lasso swinging around Clope's neck. It ended with him being sidelined in time for a bull to stampede over him. Robert angled towards me and grinned at Clope. He was putting on a show, apparently.

"You could always step in for me. I would pay you double what you're being paid at Vogue. You look like you could manage my office very well." Clope grinned in the background. His overgrown belly shaking with laughter.

"Ok, I'll bite Robert. And what exactly would I be doing?" Defiant anger started to bubble up and spill over from me.

"Running errands, office stuff, short trips, keeping my diary in check, paperwork, shopping, company, holiday booking." Robert leaned back in his chair and put both his hands behind his head. Clope laughed heartily, and I moved my head away from him slightly. Robert let out a wicked chuckle as he watched me squirm.

"Well, you might be paying double, but that position needs to pay triple. Plus, I get great clothes already at Vogue without all the drama," I snapped back. Livid with him trying to proposition me. I flicked my ebony hair out of my face.

"Seriously, that's what you're worried about? I would give you a clothing allowance. It would be substantial. Give it some thought," he pandered softly.

Robert flipped over a business card to me. "Be sure to call the office if you're interested. I can set up an interview," he added softly.

"And what's wrong with your current assistant?" I posed.

"She doesn't have your sharp eye and great wit. I saw what you did at the model shoot. You did great." Robert winked, and beamed his killer-watt millionaire smile at me. He was watching my work. He knew. Secretly, I was happy with the compliment. Let me dig a little deeper and change the subject.

"So Clope, how do you and Robert know one another?" Wait for it...

"Ah - ya know I work on investments, that type-a thing. I manage the properties and extensive portfolio that the Elliots have. I'm-a bricks and mortar guy," he replied.

"I see." I dared to look into the eyes of a killer. In the corners they were bloodshot, with yellow stains around them. His eyes were so dark with evil his eye color couldn't be distinguished. Black like his heart, I imagined. Made me push back my seat from him for some reason. I don't know how Mrs. Brazil could even be comfortable in his presence.

The killer continued. "If you're ever in the market for a house or investment, just get in touch. I'll help you out. Always good to have real estate, eh Robert?"

"Indeed. A solid investment and one that yields good returns, if done right." *I bet you take care of real estate. Just happens to be that people represent the properties.* I nodded my head in fake acknowledgment. I considered how it could be an important move for the case to be so close to the inner workings of the Elliot clan. I could gain more intel at a faster rate and compile evidence. More risk and more danger. Life threatening danger. Was I willing to do that in the name of justice, or was it my ego talking?

Robert's current assistant was a leggy blonde thing, all about twenty-five at the latest. She looked like something out of the *Simply Irresistible* film clip. I spotted her on the company website. She was front and center at Robert's party. She was sucking face with some dude in a corner. There hadn't been any more conversations on the wiretap since that party last time. June 15 was fast approaching on the calendar for the drop. Soon there had to be a meeting about it. As I ruminated on this, Evana came into view. She was dressed in a purple halter neck dress which flowed out at the bottom stopping right before her knees. She looked like she just stepped out of Teen Vogue. Her lips were a frosty pink, and her eyes shimmered in bronze. She carried a fuchsia and tan Hermes leather handbag. At a guess, $18,000 laid strapped across her chest. My ability to pick brand names was getting better. Evana's hair was pulled up in a tight bun with her blue eyes shining bright. Her cheekbones sparkled with iridescent blush. Radiant. Saved by the bell once again. I found it harder and harder to fight off Robert's advances. He dialed them up a notch every time I saw him. Almost like he enjoyed toying with his prey, as a cat did to a mouse. Made me want to slap him.

"Darling, are you ok? I hope Robert looked after you. Did he tell you I was running late?" Evana hugged me before she hugged her husband. She turned to Robert and gave him a cold kiss on the cheek. He looked at her approvingly.

"Of course, I looked after her. We were just getting better acquainted," he said smoothly.

Robert ran his baby blues straight through me and curved his lips slightly. Timely, Miss Brazil arrived back with drinks in hand.

"Ola, Mami, nice to see you! You look so gorgeous." She exclaimed when she locked eyes with Evana. Miss Brazil and Evana exchanged fake air kisses. A custom I never understood. All the fluff and pretenses. She was giving off Hollywood vibes. Yes. I determined there were Hollywood people at this party. Fly-ins.

"How was the shoot? Was Miguel the photographer? He does such great work." Ah, the leggy Brazilian must be a model, too. They worked together. Evana looked at me to explain.

"Claudia worked on a swimsuit issue with me. My gawd, how freezing was it in the Archipelagos? Remember that?" Evana waved her hand like it was old news. *Half your luck to be whining about a swimsuit shoot in the Archipelagos.* I felt inferior around all these models. I mean, I got my swimsuit online and it worked for me. Covered the bits I needed it to. I worked out regularly, so it wasn't like I was unfit. Plus, I had to run from or catch bad guys on occasion. Not so much lately. I had been paper pushing, and this was my first time in a while getting back into the mix. This case was testing me. I was in uncharted waters.

I heard Evana and Miss Brazil chatting about the shoot. My focus drifted elsewhere. Robert and Clope moved slightly away and were whispering something closer to the edge of the pool. Robert's hands were becoming animated, and he appeared to be angry. He ran his hand through his hair and a prominent vein became visible in his neck. The whispering escalated to fury.

"Fix it, Clope! That's what I pay you for." I caught the tail end of the conversation. Were they running behind schedule? Had something gone wrong with a shipment? *What was it related to?*

Evana swept me away from my thoughts.

"Sara, how are you? How'd you like the shoot the other day? You're really getting the hang of it now. Maybe I do want you around after all." She gave a wry smile. Well, if private investigation didn't work out, at least I knew I was a shoo-in for being a Vogue intern.

"I was happy with how it all went on the shoot. Fun experience." I wasn't lying at all. I really did have fun at the shoot. Evana stared over at Robert with a look I couldn't decipher. She inclined my way and whispered.

"He's not the guy you think. Clope gives me the creeps. He's sleazy. I didn't tell you the other day I heard him talking about this deal he's got going on. I mean Robert always has deals going down. I don't get involved, you know?" Evana scrunched her face in a weird way. Her slender fingers were coated with a turquoise nail polish, and she was visibly shaking. She sounded like she had more to say, so I listened.

"He told me to keep my nose out of it otherwise there would be trouble. But I smelt a lotta bullshit. Always working and cutting deals. Something feels different this time. I'm scared." Evana let out a troubled laugh. I didn't want to stop her talking, so I nodded for her to continue.

"So, I just shut up you know?" I pursed my lips together. The lives of billionaires. If only the world knew what went down behind the veil.

"Did they have a code word they used for the deal?

Anything weird?" I had earned Evana's trust, so I tested the waters for more specific questions.

"I don't know... something like Slick Rick. I gotta get a drink. I'm wiped out today." Evana mumbled, cricked her neck and headed off to the table where the drinks were.

Just the confirmation I was searching for. Reviewing all the details, here's what I had so far: a garbage bag with a body according to Evana; a code for what I assumed to be a drug deal; Hawk in on the operation separately that related to my case; Clope, the goon; Colombians at the party cutting deals – no connection to the actual case I was hired to solve. This was bigger than I thought, and I was determined to get to the bottom of it. *Fast.*

8

HAWK

ive a.m. coffee at my favorite little corner of the earth. A place where I could be incognito. One of those early openers for a morning caffeine hit right after a killer gym session. A phone call from my protégé, Sara. From my research and talking to Clemens, Elliot was in the midst of running a major drug deal from a Columbian import. *Suarez.* The deal was set in motion for June 15th. *Piece of cake.* Only thing left to do was find out how far Elliot's reach penetrated the police department. If I didn't, the clown would get off again and pay off more jokers. The vicious cycle would continue.

I was feeling twisted inside about hiding certain parts of the case, but I knew it was best. Evana was still hanging in there with this dickweed. The love bug had caught up and sunk its claws into me. I was greatly affected. I may have driven by Evana's photo shoot. I may have even arranged a bottle of Moet to be dropped off by courier. She loved her Moet; she liked the sound when the cork popped. I knew she would enjoy the card I wrote even more. I got the shop clerk to pen the card with my message. My handwriting wasn't the neatest. The message was innocent enough, and when Evana got it she would know that I sent it. I *had* to watch the courier deliver it. Ashamed to say, I hacked into the FedEx system. I found out the delivery guy's name. Plus the route he was on to make sure it arrived. Watching from the sidelines... I was becoming obsessed, scaring even myself with the depth of my love for her.

I wanted to see her face, that's all. I was justifying the reasons in my head. I sat across the way from the venue, watching. Don't ask me about how I found out about her shoot. *Ask no questions and I will tell you no lies.* She was in her fluffy dressing gown when she came out in the open. Between outfits changes, I sensed. She was more breathtaking than when I was with her. I wished I could take her in my arms at that moment. I felt a tug on my heart. It was almost too much. *Almost.* The urge was strong to walk onto the photo shoot set and - *do what Hawk?* Interrupt her work? I was bugging. My left brain kicked in thankfully, holding me captive in my seat. I wanted to shout from the rooftops the truth about who I was. I felt like I could trust her. I guess she made her choice at the end of the day. I was this unknown half spy, half assassin living between worlds. It wasn't a steady basis for a healthy relationship... *unless I told her, and she was down with it. I could bring her into my world. I knew she could handle it. How to break it to her though?*

The photo shoot was by a poolside with large beach balls. Looked like a Vogue summer shoot. Evana was facing me. I observed her from across the street in a new pick-up truck. A different vehicle than the one I normally drove so she wouldn't notice. The FedEx guy dropped it off. I had my surveillance gear pick up the conversation. More guilt set in. But I had to see her reaction. *Needed to.* Wanted to see her face light up.

"Evana, urgent package for you! Gurl, you are winning

hearts wherever you go!" A curvy Afro American stylist in a blue smock came with the package, waving it in her hand like a wand. Evana spun around to receive the package, a look of elation filling her face. She opened it: a bottle of Moet. I watched her jaw drop. When I brought her Moet during our relationship, I put a blue ribbon around it. My own touch. Obviously, she saw the blue ribbon. I could tell. A double take... The African-American stylist chimed in.

"Evana, is everything alright?" Evana swung around violently, looking around the venue. I was watching her behind the gates.

"Is he here? Oh my God, is he here?" Evana shrieked.

"Is who here, baby? Ain't nobody here but us and this here bottle of Moet! And Miguel for the shoot, of course," she responded, eyeing the bottle.

Evana clutched her chest, pulling her white dressing robe together. A horrified look of shock crossed her face. She knew it was me. That wasn't the reaction I was hoping for. But hey, at least she knew I was thinking of her. I wanted her to enjoy her life. I meant her no harm. I wanted her to smile when she saw the bottle. Maybe it was time to truly let it go. The connection had been severed. This existence I lived was perilous, anyway. It had a perverse stranglehold on my psyche. I didn't know how to live a normal civilian life. I had seen so much in my military journey that this was the only way for me to reconcile it.

Sara rang not long after wanting to meet. She was a hell of an investigator. It was going to be a little harder to get her off my case on this one. *Why was she getting so involved with Evana anyway?* Cared way too much, but given my stalker capacities that was the pot calling the kettle black.

I found out from my trusted street sources that the Columbian coke drop off was a much bigger deal after all. It was climbing in the money stakes. Up to 30 million. The Columbians lost a supplier on the west side of New York due to a breakdown in communications. The supplier couldn't clean the money quick enough, was the word from my informant. A new street player was in town, and bricks were moving fast. No point tipping the cops on it. This was a case-building exercise. The feds never wanted the little guy unless they thought he might snitch and talk about their bosses. These types of cases took time to percolate.

On my end, the Secret Intelligence Service (SIS) sought my input, and a guaranteed result. A guy named Clope was uncovered on my wiretap. I heard him talking at the pool party. Could see him, too. Sara sent across the photo cred to me. She got him clean and square on the little spy camera I gave her. Raspy-toned guy with a face that resembled a smushed sandwich. A face only a mother could love. Some sort of prototype talks were going on. Sara told me she caught the tail end of the conversation, and the talks were heated between Elliot and Clope poolside.

I had the equipment where I could peep a visual on this guy and track his daily movements. I didn't have the sharpest details, but new developments were forming. Clope, and another - tall skinny bald guy – hauled a kid from Scafen State School in a black jeep yesterday at three p.m. The kid looked like he just shat the bed when they pulled him in. I ran a background check. The kid's name was Dean Noble, the highest-grade point average in the school. Not so unusual, except his scores were at genius level, and he was only fifteen. He wasn't staying at the State school for long. He was heading to Harvard to form part of the technology team there. A good-looking kid in a nerdy sort-a way. His genius was all over the local papers. The kid was a scientific and mathematical pro. He had a background and fascination with drone and aircraft surveillance.

It was a brisk Friday morning when I tuned into the radio satellite connection wired in my van. It was staticky, but enough to hear what was being said. I would need to fix that at some stage. The satellite was undetectable on the roof. It sat like a flat T.V. set top box on my van roof. Anybody could walk past it. Concealed in plain sight.

"So, you got it sorted right?" They were talking to the kid.

"Errr- I had some problems with the equation, but it's starting to be clear now. The coding is going to take me a little more time to work with. The laser beams seem to work pretty well." Pause. "Who did you say you guys work for? I shouldn't be doing this... It looks like it's highly classified stuff. I don't feel good about it." I winced when he said that. The kid's voice was high pitched, he sounded shit-scared. Poor bastard. If it went down, I would make a move, though.

Raspy dude spoke. *"I don't give a fuck if you feel good or not. Your mother won't be feeling good if you disappear, either. Will she? Just do what we ask, and nobody needs to get hurt."*

"Err- when you put it like that I guess so. I need a couple more days to look at the wiring of the prototype. The reason it didn't work for them was because they didn't have enough satellite range. They couldn't gain a clear picture. They didn't test it for key components. I need to set it on a section of the city to see. It will be ready to test run on Sunday, if I can just hack into the central mainframe unit and reprogram. I can redirect it to this satellite. They have some sort of code blocker on it."

"Whatever. You just better not be playing with us kid. Because if I find out you are, you won't make it to see your 16th birthday," the terror warning came.

"That would be a shame – I had a big party planned." *Kid you're killing it.* I cringed, that wouldn't go down well with Smushface. Clope and the bald guy pushed the kid out of the car two blocks away from the school. The kid rolled out like a tumbleweed. He got up and dusted his jeans off. The sleek black vehicle rolled away from the school at a tepid pace.

I had enough intel to scope out the next steps. Get to the prototype before the kid finishes. Get it back to the unit it belonged to, and my job was done. Eight figures to be deposited into my bank account. That's provided I completed the mission alive. Might take off somewhere for a while. Reset myself and sharpen my skills. The timing would probably be right to pay a visit to the Chief at the reservation.

Inconvenient memories were fading in and out of my system. I kept witnessing Evana's face. A replay fluctuating on loop from the early days of our relationship. Evana with her delicate strands of blonde hair, soft like a baby's. I remembered the way it used to drift across my face as I slept. Annoyed me at time. Now I wished for it back. Slender arms wrapped around my back, that were there when I woke up. *God, I missed that.* She had rocked every part of my life, but in a good way. I hadn't ever considered love to be that important. Unless women were army brats like me, I didn't see how it was possible. I did try a couple of times with a few military ladies... Never worked out. I would get stationed or flown out of the country somewhere, and the connection would be lost. Because of that, I never let my feelings run too deep, and neither did they. They were dedicated to their military service, just like I was. No harm. No foul. And no double-crossing. But Evana. She left an imprint on my soul so deep, I was terrified it would never be released.

9

SARA

♟

"So, my friend, how goes it? Any developments on the case?" Hawk was at my place and we were working through the case, munching on nachos. Detective and assassin food.

"Yeah, I got a couple of things. One is for Evana – I'm worried about her. Another is for the case itself." I crunched a Dorito between thoughts. Hawk raised his eyebrows as I continued. "Yeh, this Clope guy from the pool party... They were in a hush-hush conversation about something. A proto-type, that's my first solid lead about the case. I can see how they may have been working with Michael Sawyer. Now it's time for the why."

"Exactly." Hawk responded. He was throwing back a beer with his nachos. "Keep going."

"Sawyer worked in the software department. He wasn't a standout or anything. Just a normal dude with tech skills. However, if Elliot sought him out, then obviously he had a mighty special skill set. I was thinking of paying a visit to his wife. Ask her if she knew what he was working on."

"Sounds like a good move. You got it." Hawk responded. I kept my detective thoughts flowing.

"Clope was the guy I picked up after the first party on the surveillance. The job is going down on June 15th. Think we can tip the feds? I have the list of the cops in the Narcotics Division. Any chance you can flesh out from your sources who's clean?"

"Yeah, I can run a scan. See if they've been disciplined or warned. See if anything sticks out. Let me work on that." Hawk's chin dripped with excess cheese. I pointed at it.

"You got a little something right there." He swatted my hand playfully, wiping it off with his napkin.

"I got it. I got it."

"No location yet. I'm waiting. They're speaking in code, though. Slick Rick, and I'm not sure the address is coming in plain speak, either. I mean they might have some other method. Evana confirmed to me they speak in code. She has a *lot* of casual information. She drops it when she's drunk or high. Robert's good. I haven't heard anything on the wiretap the last couple of days, which I find strange. That date is coming up real fast," I added with concern. Hawk had a grimace on his face. I knew that face. It means he knows something. He had that same look when he found out an undercover agent in Cabo sent a hitman to have him taken out. "What do you know, Hawk? Talk to me," I pressed him.

"I don't know as much as you think. Maybe a common link. You know the drill."

"Right now, it's a need to know basis," we both chimed in unison.

"I do know that, but you need to tell me enough so I can cover my ass," I reasoned. Hawk sometimes withheld information from me as a form of protection. I was well capable of taking care of myself. I found him to be downright frustrating at times. I had no intention to foil his plans or mark, but a sneaking suspicion made me think that's what he believed.

"I won't leave you hanging. I just don't want you impli-cated any more than you have to be," he reasoned.

"Ok." As much as I was hesitant about Hawk's methods, he'd given me every reason to trust him. His report probably told him not to speak. The thing to me was, where was the information going? It was just me and him. Hawk has serious trust issues, if you ask me.

"The Clope guy is a problem, and he's one of Robert's goons. That much I know for sure," he confirmed.

"I can agree with you on that. Guy's got a rap sheet that has holes in it and doesn't include half of what he's done. His connection with Robert has silenced a lot of people, particu-larly in the department. You got that Cabo face again," I observed.

"Well that was a different story..." Hawk explained with ease.

I threw my hands up. "No, it's not! I could have helped you if you'd have told me what the 411 was!" He really was a lone ranger. If he let me in, we could be a real powerhouse of a team.

"I was protecting you. I didn't want you to get hurt. Plus, I had it handled. You would have had blood on your hands. My contacts would have implicated you in the case. They don't mind a double-cross," he affirmed in a calm voice.

"Alright, alright – you win." I put my palms up in mock surrender.

"Too right, Sista."

I laughed. "Hawk, you are annoying, but you would tell me if it was going to be anything crucial to the case, right?" I knew I was repeating myself. I just wanted to get it through his thick skull.

"No doubt. So, you said you had something else? Evana?" He breezed right into the next subject.

"Yeah, I'm worried she's in immediate danger. I can't have

her coming up missing. I need to keep her alive." I paused. "Oops. That didn't sound good."

"Well, it's the truth. The reason why you went undercover in the first place. To infiltrate. She's got the juice, as you said," Hawk reasoned.

"I wanna see if it's anything serious or just some dumbass messing around. She was talking to me about this guy. First comes a black rose being delivered, and then she received a bottle of Moet with a blue ribbon. She said it was from this ex that she used to date. She looked scared. Can you run a fingerprint dust-up on this card? I mean, I would do it myself, but I have a lotta work to do on this case."

"Sure, let me look into it and I'll get it back to you." Hawks eyes lowered, his voice was even, but something... A hint of a flicker across his face. *What was that? The same flicker I saw when I mentioned Evana's name last time.*

"So, any breaks in your side of the case?" I switched subjects for some reason.

"Yup, I have one thing left to do and I've got the lead to complete it." Hawk studied me closely.

"Your report? Is it before the drop you have to report?" I was gently probing him now. He gave me a slow smile.

"Just work on finding out about Sawyer. See if you can find any paper trails to link Elliot's company to his." Hawk looked at me with intensity. "I got your back. You know that, right?"

"For sure I know that. I just wish sometimes you would let me in on operations a little more. It's my case, after all." Resentment mounted at the pit of my stomach. I pressed it down for now.

"Look, if I tell you now, you will end up down a rabbit warren. I need you to stay focused on your end. Things will come together – you'll see. Plus, like I said, I don't want you in any situation where you can be implicated."

"Implicated? Hawk, we are working this case right now

together in my kitchen! If that's not implication, I don't know what is." I sighed heavily; Hawk tipped my nose lightly. I wrinkled it at him in frustration. Same thing Evana did to Robert when he expressed frustration. Interesting.

"Certain parts. If you were questioned by these guys, they would break you. But there's nothing to worry about, because the job is almost done from my end." I left it. I didn't want to fight with him about it anymore. The stubborn mule wouldn't budge anyway.

"You might want to check Robert's hard drive; he might have some information or a file about the case. See if you can check his office again. Look for dates."

"Hmm he did offer me a job... I can technically get in there with his consent. Other than that, there's no way in hell that will be easy. He was edgy last time I entered the office."

"Might be a faster way to check out the scene... What's happening with the cover at Vogue?"

"Well, it could work that I ditch that and work directly with Robert. I want to have a few degrees of separation from him so I could work on Evana. We seem to have formed a bond."

Hawk coughed. "Stay neutral, Sara. That's the only way you can protect her. Do your job." Hawk's voice was stern.

"She seems to have two dudes that are causing her problems." I drifted off in thought.

"Sucks to be her." Hawk mumbled under his breath as he drained the last of his beer. *What was up with him?* He seemed so moody about the case... Dropping little horse pellets here and there. I would sniff out what was going on one way or another. Mark my words. I had a nose for when I was being fed manure.

♟

Two days later at the mansion of all mansions, another Elliot party. Another invite. Poolside drinks again in the backyard. Sophisticated crowd, minimal drugs that my eye could capture, anyway. I walked around to the back gate like last time. I had the walk-in procedure down pat. Give over the phone and security check. I made my way to the free-standing bar set up by the pool. The bartender handed me a cold white wine. I took the first cool sip quickly to ease my jangled nerves. Ah, so good. Meanwhile my shoe got caught on something in the process, it seemed. It felt heavy to lift from the ground. Gum. *Dammit!* I kept looking at it. I wasn't paying attention to what or who was in front of me while I tried to lift out of the stickiness. While I was wrestling with the gum serpent from my shoe, the swearing commenced. My drink was dangerously close to spilling over. Next thing I know I face planted right into a rock-hard chest marinating in musky undertones. I added a splashed drink on the rock-hard chest for good measure.

Shit!

Robert. He gripped both my arms near the elbows. My drink still had a few drops in the glass. A heat wave of desire hit me so quick, it made me want to melt into his embrace and lock lips. Some sort of wicked spellbinding energy is what he possessed. *Was I completely insane?* I tried to move quickly and pull back. His grip on my elbows was too firm. With a crooked smile, the next move was his. A warm kiss on the cheek ran desperately close to the edge of my mouth, which was open. He dropped my elbows after that, and I put the drink down on the nearest counter.

"Mm mm. You smell amazing. Sweet."

"I'm sorry! I didn't realize you were there." I aimlessly rubbed his chest out of nervousness where the drink spilled. I deeply regretted that. I felt the shape of his pectorals defined beneath my padded fingertips. The touch was brief, but enough to set me on fire. Elliot was in magnificent shape.

"That's ok, no harm done – means I have to get changed. If I knew I was going to receive this level of attention, I would've hoped you split something on me earlier." Robert laughed with ease.

"I'll be sure not to spill anything on you again. That's for sure." I murmured and looked away. Robert caught what I said, his face dancing with easy laughter.

"Excuse me for a minute, Sara. I'll be back." He winked at me, then in a flash was gone.

I felt like a giddy schoolgirl. I needed to find the closest bathroom there was. Just to escape the erotic feelings billowing inside of me. Seemed impossible to keep them tempered. Almost like a nightmarish vixen had taken residence over my senses, but only when I was in his presence for some reason.

Welcome to the dark side it said... Kiss him! Walk on the wild side, Sara. You're too straight anyway. You know you wanna. I shook my head desperately wanting to release the thought.

"You ok?" Robert was beside me and back from the bathroom in another white shirt. He was staring at me with great interest.

"Yeah, I'm good." I smoothed down my hair and flashed him a tight smile.

"It's okay, you know, to spill a drink on me. Usually it's not an accident." Robert spoke in a low husky tone. I arched my brows at him. His icy blue eyes were normally cool, today I felt the fiery haze in them.

"So, Robert, have you seen Evana?" Subject change ought to take the heat out of the situation.

"You seem to always be asking about my wife." Robert circled a finger overhead to indicate Evana's whereabouts, somewhere in the stratosphere.

"You know, just checking," I replied quickly.

"You're getting along well, I see. My question is why I don't seem to know so much about you, Sara?"

I dodged the question. "Well she invited me here, that's all. Always like to greet the person who invites me."

"Uncomfortable, Sara? You seem to not like being alone with me." Robert lowered his gaze. He was taller than me, so he was looking down into my eyes. He was so close I could feel his breath. The imp was in my ear again.

Ain't he sexy? Wouldn't you like to be the one in his bed? Just for one night. He didn't bump into you for no reason.

"My offer still stands, Sara. I can do for you what Vogue has, times ten. You can shop anywhere you want." His hot breath lingered, seeping into my pores. I was sure of it. I looked up and out to the party just so I could break Robert's psychological hold.

Wouldn't you like him to lick your neck, Sara? That's what you want, right? Tell him! You want him to lick in other places, too, yeh? Tell him! The imp imposter raged in full force today. I closed my eyes momentarily, furiously wanting to shut it up.

"I like the job, actually. Always something different to do each day. I get to meet fabulous models and learn about fashion. What's not to love?" Elliot narrowed his eyes at me. I don't think he bought it. Plus, my voice elevated to a shrill tone I wasn't familiar with.

I thought I would play a little game of my own. Gain a little control back that was fast sifting through my fingers.

"Tell me, Robert, how does one build an empire like yours? Did you inherit it, or is it just good ol' fashioned hard work?"

Robert studied my face. "Money equals power, power equals influence, and influence changes the game. Understand?"

"Well, that's a mouthful." I took a sip of my now half full glass.

"I could respond to that, but I'll let it slide for now." *Oh, we're playing now...*

"Would you say you like to wield your power for good or evil?"

Robert's deathly smirk indicated everything I wanted to know, his baby blue icicles sending chills straight to my core.

"Depends what the situation calls for. I'm a businessman at the end of the day. But sometimes you have to let people know where you stand.

"What about you, Miss Sara? You got a wicked side?" He was enjoying the game.

"Wouldn't you like to know, Robert," I responded, slowly taking a coquettish sip of my wine.

"Yes, I would. My sense is you do, deep down." He leaned forward then; his next move unpredictable. His menacing lips swiped the top of my earlobe. The delicate wind cooled the saliva he left there. Marking his territory. My feet didn't let me move for some reason. Rooted to the ground. *Did that just happen?* For the life of me, I don't know why I remained still. Frozen in disbelief, perhaps. My throat felt like it was in a vice grip. The words wouldn't move, either.

"I do like a challenge – that's for sure." That throaty voice was a massive turn on for me and I was growing weak. I was treading in dark murky waters. This game wasn't my forte, *but boy did I want to learn the ropes.*

"Remember Evana, your wife?" My feeble attempt to work at evening up the scoreboard.

"You know, if I want something 99% of the time, I get it. The 1% sometimes means I have to wait. Delayed gratification type of thing. I sense it's the latter with you. Dare you to play nice. But that wouldn't be any fun now, would it? Me, I rather like the build-up of tension you're creating between us."

"No, Robert, I'm not going to make you wait. Because I'm the other percentage you didn't account for. That doesn't give a flying fuck who you are. Here's one bed notch you won't be getting." My tone tumbled out spicy; I held my ground. Robert said nothing. I watched him. He seemed bemused.

"You just keep getting more and more interesting, Sara. Makes me like you even more. Trust me, you wouldn't be a bedpost. We have something deeper going on." His tone was surprisingly soft. I was becoming exasperated and turned on at the same time, mass confusion oscillating in my brain cells. I had to get away with the quickness.

Stage left, Evana was present: a little tipsy, her hair disheveled, laughing to herself like a wounded hyena. She propped herself up on the nearest barstool. Red-rimmed eyes looked back at me, one purple earring hung in her ear. God knows what happened to the other one. She was wearing a black dress with a salacious slit on the side. She had a great set of legs, so no problem there. Her go-to red ruby nails and slender fingers were grappling with a half full martini glass. The martini glass was winning. She was barely able to see the glass as she balanced it on the table. It landed in place with a burst of what looked to be either gin or vodka. An olive floated at the bottom of it. I assumed the drink to be gin. *Shaken and stirred.*

An instant stormfront of fury crossed Robert's handsome face. Hushed tones and scrutinizing looks were cast in Evana's direction. But only for the blink of an eye, then guests went back to their drinks like they hadn't just witnessed a runaway train wreck.

Oh, it's just that model.

Evana giggled and cupped Robert's face.

"Hi hi, baby! What's wrong?" She went into Marilyn Monroe pout mode. Robert jerked his face away from her.

"You're what's wrong. Get your shit together!" he hissed. "I have important people here tonight, and I don't need you off your fucking face. Don't embarrass me, Evana." Veins started to surface. The angry side of Elliot. I was still locked in the same spot, a spectator in the show.

"Here, take this and sober up now." He handed Evana a

vial of something, in a discreet way. She was barely able to grasp it in her slender fingers.

"Watch her, will you?" Robert walked away like he wanted to wash his hands of her.

I watched him move through the partygoers. From my initial head count looked to be about a hundred people in his back-yard. Evana turned her head and sniffed the vial of stuff. Her pupils morphed from huge saucers to small saucers. A change came over Evana which was hard to describe. A twisted version of sober. Ten seconds later, she let out a whooshing noise.

"Whoa – that was heavy. Ok, I'm good."

"Sara, you look amazing, and you smell delicious." I watched on in observation. *What was going on with her today?*

Evana's nose ran into my neck and she sniffed, giggling some more. She touched her nose, as if she was checking if it was still there.

"I'm sorry, I didn't mean that." She smiled strangely.

"What was that you took just now?" Investigation mode, I snatched the vial from Evana. It had a couple of drops in it. The liquid was violet purple.

"Heyyy! Give it back." Evana tried to reach out and retrieve the vial, but she was unsteady and missed me completely. I stepped out of the way and she stumbled.

"What is this?" I yelled. I looked around quickly to check nobody heard.

"Alright! Geez, relax. It's a stimulant that helps you perk up. I'm good now, *really good*." She sniffed and wiped her nose with the back of her hand.

It pained me to see her like this with Robert feeding her with a vial like that. He incited me with anger, reminding me of the reason I pursued the course of justice in the first place. I had never been enamored by a suspect. It was a disturbing situation for me. Even more reason to keep my distance. To keep working undercover at Vogue. I feared becoming unhinged by him. The vixen was reveling in the show and wanted to showcase her talents. *Couldn't hurt, could it?*

We were standing off to the side, slightly out of earshot of the partygoers.

"What's going on with you?" My eyes were running over her. Searching for an answer.

"I need some help. I heard something..." Evana's eyes were threatening to overflow with tears. Her slender hands trembled so much I had to grab them to calm her.

"Talk to me."

"I'm so dead, I'm so dead, I'm so dead." Evana started rocking back and forth on her heels with her arms crossed. I was starting to get worried about the situation.

"Talk to me, Evana. What's going on?" I looked deep into her eyes, holding her by the shoulders. Another scan of the crowd. We weren't being watched. People were too into their own cliques.

"My father, my father... He *killed* my father!" Her voice grew in volume as I scrambled to hush her.

"Shhh! Keep your voice down! Come over here!" I pulled her back further away from the crowd towards a deckchair in a secluded section of the party. The party was moving and grooving without a care. The DJ had launched into a new set of music as the sun dived into dusk.

"How do you know that?" I questioned.

"I overheard him talking to that bastard Clope about my father. How... how... he didn't want another mistake to happen." Evana's chest started heaving as the sobs overtook her. "And to have a dirty mess to clean up." Breakthrough. Another murder. *Shit*. This case was the motherload of fuckery. The attraction to Robert exited from my body like a virus that didn't belong.

"Are you a hundred?" I looked into her eyes.

What was the connection? My mind filtered all this information at a rapid rate.

"Evana, why would Robert want to kill your father?"

"My father owned the shipping yard on 84th Dock..." She was sniffling, grasping her words together. I gave her time.

"He was having trouble before he died, and some heavies were asking him to leave. They offered a large sum of money; he didn't take it." *Ahhhh, shit. Elliot.*

"They ruled my father's death a suicide. I knew my father would kill himself. The whole thing felt like bullshit to me. He was happy and proud of what he'd built. Worked there since 1985." Evana was still sobbing and breaking down. I let her go and waited for her to carry on. I watched diligently to see if Elliot or his goons were anywhere around.

"Through the strikes and lay-offs he worked damn hard." Evana wiped her hands over her face furiously a few times. I grabbed her hand to soothe her. Now I knew why she had laughed like a hyena. She had just discovered she was sleeping with the enemy.

"Wow." I had no words. Just next steps to lock this guy up and put away the key.

"Do you have any proof of overhearing the conversation?"

"I don't have shit, but I know I'm going to die." I wouldn't put anything past Robert now I knew this. I surveyed the room, scouting for Robert. I couldn't spot him. My heart picked up in pace. Ka boom. Ka boom. The beat of it ringing in my ears. Ok, coast looked like it was clear, but I knew Elliot had tentacles everywhere. Cameras on the right-hand side of the pool and the left side. I couldn't see how far they reached. Maybe we wouldn't be caught on them.

Should I tell her? Now was the time. It was an incredible risk. I probably didn't think it through enough.

"Evana, I'm a private detective and Robert is being investigated for murder, money laundering, and running a major drug ring syndicate."

"I knew it!" Her voice went up two notches. Evana's eyes

were almost bugging out of her head. Her fists balled up by her sides.

"Shhh!!" I reigned her in.

"You're no Vogue girl. I knew from day one." Was it that obvious I wasn't into the fashion world?

"Well thanks, but I think I held my own," I countered.

"It's too late. Robert saw me, I think. I can't be sure, but I think he knows I overheard him. I'm dead. I'm dead." I saw the fear locked in her eyes. The lost hope.

"You're not a cop, are you? Robert has half the city on his payroll anyway, so it's not going to matter. I'm screwed!"

"No, I'm not a cop, and I'm aware. Hey, listen, we're going to bust him. It's only a matter of time." She was frantic and wouldn't settle. She started pacing around in a circle. What could I expect? She just found out her father was killed by her own husband.

"If Robert finds out about you..." She started waving her hands.

"Evana, look at me. You have got to calm down so I can help you! Smile. Pretend we're having a normal conversation. We got this," I hissed.

"O-ok." She closed her eyes and breathed in. A tear trickled down her cheek.

"He's not going to find out. We are going to maintain the status quo until I know more. I have a source that can back us up if the shit hits the fan." I watched her tears fall to the ground and Evana swipe them away.

"He has eyes everywhere. You don't know." Her lip quivered with dread.

"Sit tight and act like you didn't hear anything at all. Can you do that, Evana?" I found strength in that moment I wasn't sure was mine. At this point, the gloves were off.

Evana lit up a cigarette shakily. "Yeh, I think so."

"You'll protect me, right?" Cat was out of the bag now. My cover was entirely blown. Let's just hope that didn't come back to bite me in the ass. Felt like the right thing to do at the time.

"I will make sure nothing happens to you, Evana. Promise." Honestly, to make that statement was heavy. I had no real idea if I could keep her safe. But Hawk could. I would put my last dollar on that. Got me thinking about my sometime sidekick, Hawk. *Time to call in the heavyweight.*

Evana ran her slender finger through her messy hair. "This is so fucked up, fucking sadistic prick! He knew about my father. I think I'm going to be sick." Evana was shaking with fury, hatred and fear, all in one breath.

If I could get to my surveillance gear, I could pick up that conversation and verify the sources. This would be a major break in the case. Justice was being paved for Mr. Playboy's downfall. This would add to the long list of crimes he deserved to be pinned for.

Just a matter of time.

10

ELLIOT

♟

Huh. Sexy, understated, classy, wound tighter than a coiled spring. *Sara.* I let her name twist over on my tongue. *Sara.* Nothing like the others. A new feeling I held for her. Not easy to describe. But very, very appealing to my appetite. More information was required first. *Who was she?* Suddenly, this woman shows up working at Vogue. She wasn't the fashion type, completely a fish out of water. That's why I asked her to work in the office. That tilted chin of defiance drove me wild. Let me get closer to her. Might be just the thing to quench my thirst for a while. I'm not a man for attachments, unless it was in the order I liked. Power, money, status, and sex. The major themes of my life. Just the way I liked it. Control was mine then. No vulnerable weaknesses being exposed. Those elements of my life I mastered. The love emotion wasn't one of them. That was a foreign concept to me. She made me rethink that...

Sara. I'm a man of endless sins, and I dance with the devil. We could never be.

She was a little too sharp, a little too observant. She wasn't into the party scene, yet was at every one of my parties of late. I knew when I was being played. Being a man of the game myself I knew when a snake slid amongst the grass. Thankfully, as a lover of chess, she just didn't know she was to be the pawn. Interesting how eager she was for a grand tour, especially to my office.

I was going to find out more about this elusive Sara. Uncover her secrets before she unearthed mine. I started the hunt by ringing an old friend in the department: everyone called him Deuce. He was a trump card up my sleeve. Deuce had orchestrated many a cover up for me: police reports mysteriously going missing along with crucial evidence. Cases getting thrown out. Witnesses disappearing. All I had to do was hand my old buddy a fat wad of cash padding his wallet. *Money could buy anything.* That method of operation was not working for him anymore. Deuce had been in the force as the New York State Police Superintendent for twenty odd years, and due to my regular cash injection Deuce was in a position to be able to retire later this year. His clearance of major drug shipments led task forces to other areas turning a blind eye, for a price. Everyone had a price. *I wondered what Sara's was...*

"Deuce, old buddy." Deuce wasn't happy to speak to me these days, now that his retirement was looming. But Deuce would do what I wanted.

"What do you want, Elliot? I thought I told you not to call me on this phone," Deuce punched out.

DEUCE WAS a steely cop who moved with purpose. The years of gritty cases were worn on his face. Lines were etched deep in his forehead; lucky he still had a mop of sandy blonde hair tousled with grey. He kept in good shape - which was unseen in his department. Most could be seen at Dunkin Donuts. In fact, he used to bond with Robert over workouts. They met at the gym downtown. Deuce had great instincts, and despite his dipping into the dark side with Elliot - was a helluva cop. He collected hundreds of major case hauls over the lifetime of his career. Now he was itching to leave the force for good. The cases and the long nights, stakeouts and catching fucked up drug dealers had taken their toll, and wifey was none too happy. He wanted to go to the islands and sit in a hammock for a while. Robert had offered a cruiser more comfortable path into retirement, so he took it. Exonerated years off his time in the muck. Too bad it came with dire consequences. To Robert, he had just seen the light. The path of least resistance to be on his payroll.

♟

"I NEED A FAVOR."

"Well I didn't think you were ringing to drop by for dinna," he answered in a raspy voice.

"I sense you don't like hearing from me, Deuce, but remember I hold the deuces, right? I'm sure you want a smooth run into retirement. I wouldn't want anything to jeopardize that," I said smoothly. Deuce heaved a mighty sigh into the phone.

"What can I do for you, Elliot? And next time use the secure line we talked about," he punched back.

"Yessir! I need you to check into someone for me... Ms. Sara Clemens. I need a background check. Give me some groundwork."

"Ok, give me 'til three... It's the day for low life's in here, but hey – you already know that." Was that a slight he was throwing at me?

"Careful, Deuce. Remember our agreement," I warned in a steely tone.

I knew I had Deuce by the balls. No room for wriggling from the grip here. A couple of calls, tip offs, transaction listings, some interesting photos from the strip club sent to his wife, and this whole man's life would fall apart. *Not today, though. I was feeling rather nice.*

♟

THE RICH MAHOGANY desk I owned had been passed down through generations of my forefathers. I was proud of my kin and the legacy the Elliot clan had built. A prestige line of old money, secret societies and high stakes business deals. Many of my deals were legitimate and above board.

Except I knew the secret corners of human hearts, the depravities that lurked there, the willingness of people to escape their own pain at all costs. This phenomenon crossed all barriers, young and old... I was the people's man. *Give the people what they want, right?* Feed the empty darkness of their souls like bottomless pits. The drug ring I ran in college got me through. I started it out of boredom, really. It's not like I needed the money. I was born into money. I wanted to see what I had power over. Just trying to stand out from my father's shadow, to be honest. Just an unfortunate incident that happened with the young reporter...

A little too much digging led to a single gunshot to the head, and an early grave. *What a shame.* Had to take off to Europe for a little while after that. Good times, parties, girls, classes, well paid-off lecturers and tutors for drugs worked well, got me top scores. I was smart enough without all the writing papers. More fun to have someone else do it. Having said that, I am a generous man and pay extremely well. Some tutors were able to pay off their student loans because of me.

Humans are greedy, myself included. The dorm ring worked well; it led me to some long-standing clients. Most of all, they were loyal to the dollar bill. Some I shook my head at because they reached a slippery slope, into the pits of hell. They worshipped the white powder, and its claws dug into their souls, eating away on their remains. Months and sometimes years later, people died. Yes, that professor had overdosed; that, too, was a shame. He was one of my best graders. Just meant I had to recalibrate the operation. My motto was never *ever* sample the product. I had testers for that. Lab rats I called them. That's why my extracurricular business was so successful.

Clean and efficient, my hands were kept nice and squeaky clean.

I did have that one bad batch running through the college where I was forced to recover my profits from a shitty supplier. *He also came up missing.* Reduced my goddamn campus supply rate by 38% due to overdoses. Word got out. That murder had never been discovered; the guy was a known drug runner, so nobody was missing him at this point except his family. Condolences to them. At times, sacrifices need to be made for the greater good.

Took me a year to recover my campus territory and gain trust back. By the time that debacle got cleared up, I discovered a high-grade coke supplier, jacked the prices, upping the ante by targeting the Hollywood crowd. That's when my operation really took off. *That's called smart business.* I had to hire new wings in my operations to clean my money through some clever account-keeping tactics. The operation had been under extensive expansion at a rapid rate, and major money was being channeled through my empire.

The operation had to break new ground, including a new warehouse arrangement. A place to ship and distribute. The current digs were too small, and the product was now imported from Columbia. I had airport Border Patrol operatives on my payroll, and a clear runway to allow certain products through.

Evana's father, Cluster Ferman, had been hard to handle. A blue-collar type. I had two shipping yards in perfect arrangement along the same route. We had come to certain terms with each yard. I was a businessman and wanted to support the local docks. I was reasonable. Two shipping yard foremen had agreed to turn a blind eye to certain inspections of a certain product. To call off the sniffer dogs when my shipment came in. The foremen offered safe houses for temporary placement of the product. They supplied drivers who knew no better to run shipments in and out. No questions asked, and all for a small dock fee. Small for me, but a small fortune for these individuals.

Cluster Ferman, however, was a battle-axe thirty years in the shipping yard game.

"Eat shit. I'm not clearing your product." Those were his exact words. Brought a smile to my face.

He came up from a young pup to the head honcho through sheer guts and determination. *I liked him - until I didn't.* He was an Eastern Bloc European, so he had experienced cold winters, communism, union strikes and bloodshed on the yard. Cluster had seen it all. He wouldn't stand to reason, you see.

"How about a higher commission, surely we can work something out?" I tried to coax him, because I liked Cluster and felt sorry for him. I wanted him to win, I had even thought about how the nature of such a man could be utilized in my organization. Eastern Bloc countries were known for their corruption tactics. I felt like I could win Cluster over and forge a deeper business relationship. That wasn't to be, because turns out Ferman had morals, integrity, and steel balls. Two things I despised and admired at the same time.

"No fucking way. Now get the hell off my dock!"

He left me no choice. I didn't want to be hands on in the situation, so my lynchpin Clope took him out. Execution style, he was found slumped behind one the warehouse containers in the yard with a baloney sandwich next to him. *Shame.* Sucked to be Cluster. *Oh well. Gun in his hand. He committed suicide according to the records.* I always liked to know a little bit about the people I was dealing with. What more could I leverage from them? Turns out Ferman had a hottie daughter; blonde, leggy, gap in the teeth and a vulnerable look that I felt could work in my favor. She could be the next Mrs. Elliot. Maybe suppress the tiny edge of guilt I felt for this killing. Never really had an affection for my associates; a healthy dose of detachment was good business. But this one I pitied. I found out more about the leggy blonde. She was, in fact, a superstar model. The perfect trophy. We would look like the ultimate power couple. Yep – I was a bastard, but a charming one at that.

Now history was about to repeat. I was taking a stroll down memory lane reminiscing over the murder with my comparade, Clope. I was working late in the office. We were talking logistics of my largest sophisticated operation. We had come a long way. This all happened on that phone call… *I was too careless.*

A shot of peach under tones wafted past my door.

Someone was at the door while I was talking to Clope.

A flash of blonde hair, footsteps. *Evana.* I knew that scent. My wife. For now.

Couldn't risk it; time to make special arrangements. *She had to go.*

The pretty brunette could be the replacement. Always nice to have a woman occupy my bed. I grabbed my lotus paperweight in contemplation as I thought about the next move to make. My fingers flicked over the surface of the paperweight that my mother had given me when I was fifteen.

"This, my boy, is a keepsake for when you take over the throne. Always remember you're an Elliot…"

It was indeed the same paperweight used to crush a man's fingers when he dared undercut me on a deal gone bad. Big mistake. *Wait.* I twiddled the paperweight in my hands for a brief moment. A small circular object was attached underneath the paperweight. I looked at it. A fucking transmitter... I had been bugged. Few guesses as to the culprit.

SONOFABITCH...

11

SARA

♟

I always liked the soft patter of raindrops on a rooftop. They were soothing me now. Snuggled under blankets and curled up to a good book was what I wanted to do. I had a case to solve though, and things were escalating rapidly. Two unsolved murders. A drug ring. A prototype of some sort. *And a mind fuck at that.*

My neighborhood was friendly, good coffee spots, low crime rate and a mix of young and old. My surveillance tapes and recordings were set up in one corner of the house along with cameras and headphones. My backroom I used as a makeshift darkroom to develop images. Not a full-blown studio, but I did the best I could. I had a drawer of devices, one of which was a recorder disguised as a pen. *007, eat your heart out.* I had this cool, blue flower lapel that was actually a transmitter. Courtesy of Hawk. Paperwork and case files pertaining to my client's dead son were sprawled across the kitchen table. This case had opened every other dark treasure chest that Elliot was hiding – except the one I needed to focus on: the death of Michael Sawyer. I was hoping this cookie trail was leading me to the promised land. The tricky web of entanglements in this case were trapping me like a black widow spider. Every time I tried to get out and move in one direction, a new web formed, snagging me.

I was speculating over coffee. I was about to brew some to help me trawl through the surveillance tapes. I was trying to pick up any nuances I might have missed. I had to work a plan to get the tentacles of Elliot away from Evana long enough to formulate a getaway. I had Hawk with me. Nothing was going to slip past him. I let a depleted sigh go from my lips and then the phone rang.

"Hello, Detective." Evana.

"Shhh!! Keep your voice down. Is Robert around you? We have to be very careful right now. Don't rock the boat. Are you in any immediate danger?"

"No, seems to be business as usual for the cretin. I can't stand him touching me. I see a monster every time he looks at me." I heard a slow blow out of cigarette smoke.

"Feels eerie, though, I think he knows. I have this feeling." I had to get her out of there asap. Trouble was, it was delicate. I didn't want murder number three on my watch.

"Oh, by the way. I'm planning on hiring a hitman to kill Robert." Another puff of the cigarette being blown out.

I laughed, maybe a nervous laugh. I laugh when things are too much to bear.

"Evana, let me handle it. It's my job. If you do that he's won," I said in an exasperated tone.

"Oh, what? You don't think I can do it?" She had the financial means, and the motive. The coolness of her tone is what disturbed me. At the party when she overheard the conversation, it was her hysterics that led me to break my cover. I wanted to let her know she had someone on her side. It was dawning on me that might not have been a good solution.

"I plan to play with his balls first - crush them. Then let

the hitman come in and destroy him like he's done to many others. He has so many people in this city on his payroll, it's unbelievable. He's untouchable, and not even the best detectives could catch the killer of my father. He was executed two years ago. He was so good to me." Evana started choking up on the other end of the line. "Now look. My hero is dead. The only man I ever loved." Evana growled with rage underneath her breath. Can't say I blamed her. Imagine finding out you're sleeping with the guy who killed your father. I was asking a lot from her. She sounded like she was on the verge of going bat shit crazy.

"Breathe, Evana, I want to catch him as badly as you do. We just have to do it by the book so we can put him behind bars for a *very* long time. I'm gonna get you outta there quick. I'm making the arrangements as we speak." The words tumbled out rapidly. I didn't want her to do anything rash.

"Why the hell are you on the case, then! *Where* are the cops? Let me tell you where they are. On his fucking lap! You will never catch him. I swear. He's too powerful," agonizing sobs were coming through the other end of the line. I was going to need to talk her off the ledge, figuratively speaking.

"Just like you said, a lotta dirty cops on payroll, plenty of ways to hit him," I lied. I had no idea how this case was coming together. My private client was waiting on answers from me.

"If you don't catch him and he doesn't kill me first, I am going to make sure he can never harm another person on the planet Earth, so help me God!!! You better catch him, lock him up. Otherwise I will do what I need to do," Evana shot at me bitterly as her voice croaked.

"Evana, you *need* to be careful with your phone. Eyes and ears are everywhere. Let's wrap this conversation up," I added in an anxious tone.

"It's a cheap phone. I got one today so don't worry. I'm

smart," she added with sarcasm. *Kudos*. Not just a pretty face. I was impressed.

"Ok, continue to call me on it. Make sure Robert doesn't see it."

"Alright."

"I will see you at the shoot. I will have a game plan by then."

I wanted her to wear a wire, but I knew Robert was too smart for that. He body checked his security guards on a regular basis.

Robert Elliot. Creamy, like butter. Cocky. You would think it was a turn-off. But *sadly no*, just a constant reminder of my feminine wiles being launched into orbit. I had forgotten what it was like to feel down there. I figured I was numb. I had been working cases back to back with food wrappers left over in my kitchen and empty coffee cups everywhere. I was completely immersed in my job. It took up most of my days, sometimes nights – especially if I was on a stakeout.

Couldn't just pick a single man for the heart to call. Could I? It had to be a badass wealthy son of a gun that had a penchant for play toys. He ignited the bad girl in me. This called for Ben and Jerrys. Ice cream therapy. Least the ice cream was sweet and didn't cost me my life or integrity as a woman. It came with an extra ten kilos on my waistline. Empty calorie day sounded like a good way to let myself off the hook. Maybe Ben and Jerry would provide the much-needed answers.

12

ELLIOT

♟

"Deuce, *my man*, what you got for me?"

"Ah, you wanna meet and I can hand you the file? No paper trail, I'm not sending it to you." Deuce's voice was grim.

"Send it across encrypted like we've done in the past." The way Deuce's voice sounded let me know I was right about Ms. Clemens. I was a stickler for security.

"Not that it's any of my business why you want this - ah info, but you're dealing with a live one here," he added with a hint of caution in his voice. My hands were sweaty, a little from anticipation and a little from wanting to ring Ms. Clemens neck. "Is this the secure line you're ringing me from?" Deuce sounded panicked.

"Yeah, it is. Calm down." Paranoia was setting in on the old man now he was close to retirement.

"You didn't hear it from me. The brunette used to be a photographer; now she's a P.I. and a damn good one, too. I checked her case rate, talked to a couple of people... She started her own agency three years ago..." Deuce continued, "Mother lives on Grant Terrace, parents still married, forty years together. She's single and never married. Pushing 40, obsessed with her work, highest grade point average in her school. Straight ace all the way round. Tough, persistent, like a dog after a bone. I would be careful if I were you. Never underestimate a pretty face."

"Thanks, Deuce – can always count on you to deliver. Enjoy your retirement," I said coldly.

"You betcha. Be careful, she might be the one to break your stride, Robert," he warned.

"You let me handle that, Deuce. Just concentrate on your family." He let out a gruff belly laugh at that statement.

"Will do. And Elliot..."

"Yeah?"

"No offense, but don't call my phone ever again."

I laughed hard at that. "Point taken."

I took a moment to process the information. *Well, Well, Well...*The pretty lady was a detective. This *was* going to be fun. My mouth curved in a glorious smile. That resolved the transmitter issue. Now Evana was up next.

Killing two birds with one stone. One I might play with for a while.

I was in the basement of my office underground car park downtown, ready to make an exit for the day. Before I did, though I had one more call to make.

"Clope, you know any hitters? No... I need this to be nice and clean – no mishaps. So nope, you can't do the job. You get a little messy sometimes."

"Awhh, come on boss, let me at her. This *sounds like* fun."

"I'm sure she heard me. *She knows.* She's a liability, and the brunette is a P.I. I got her covered. Don't worry about that one. Yeah...let's make it the anniversary date for her. You know the same date as her father. I think it's a nice gesture."

Clope laughed down the line. "Sure is nice of you, boss."

"Yeh, I know. That's why you like working for me, 'cos I'm a nice guy."

13

HAWK

A long cathartic run normally worked for me to get my head in a clear place. Lately it wasn't cutting the mustard. The dreams were back. *Premonitions. Evana's face screaming. I couldn't shake it. She was tied up somewhere. Ravens were flying.* A repetitive dream. It happens just like this. Same scenario with the bomb on the bus, how I first encountered Sara. How I managed to save her then.

First, it started with the ravens circling overhead in an open woodland area. The location appeared covered in fog, not clear. I saw Evana's face with a rope tied through her teeth, her hands were hog-tied in front of her. I woke up in cold sweats for two nights after that. *I had to protect her and Sara.* An intense guilt lingered in my spirit about Evana. I pushed her into Elliot's arms by not revealing my true feelings, trying to keep my double life intact.

I was in hell, this weird maze of pain. Sometimes it was in the back of my mind and didn't rise to the surface. Other times it showed up in my dreams. *You let her get away. Now karma is here.* For an occasional hired assassin that wasn't a place I wanted to be. I prided myself on not letting women distractions get in the way. It had to be this way; one wrong move and you wound up dead in my profession. If romance got too heavy or in the way of a mark, I left it.

Another drive by. *Just to check on her.* I didn't know what I was expecting to find. Felt weird doing it, even though staking out clients was part of my job description. Staking out my ex wasn't part of the plan. This time I went past Mr. Playboy's house. I thought about knocking out the cameras that were perched high up near the gate. I had a laser beam that could do that. I thought about kidnapping Evana, taking her somewhere she would never be found. For safety purposes. Elliot would come looking for sure. He wouldn't know it was me. Could be a way to lure him out. He had no clue I was part of this case. That I was watching him. This super-brat millionaire thought he had it all sewn up. There's always a dark horse in every scenario, the unseen you're not banking on.

That's part of how I got my name Hawk. The Sioux Chief on Pine Ridge Reservation initiated me into the tribe with a sacred ceremony, lots of dancing, chanting and giving thanks to the ancestors before me at the age of nine.

"I name you, Hawk. Not Little Hawk, not Big Hawk. Just Hawk. You will reach high to the heavens and see what others cannot. Use this power wisely, young one, for you will need it to fight against your enemies in the future."

May my ancestors keep me in this case. So far, they were. Giving me the signs – warnings of what was coming.

Since the high school pick up from the buffoons on the wiretap, conversations continued to fly back and forth to the boy about the satellite production. Robert's team wanted to test the equipment. It was June 10th, and in separate wire conversations their plan was to live test the prototype.

"That State Governor is a real dick, plus if the public knew what he was into he would lose his job. If only his wife knew. Hell, she might be in on it. He's getting on my goddamn nerves. Might be my first target."

First stop, the Columbians at the drop off. They were going for the double-up, two for one sale. *Coke and government satellites.* I was going to hit them with the Hawk special. I planned on alerting Sara to the murder link. She could run a paper trail.

I was due for a remote location check-in with the Secret Intelligence Service (SIS) in Prague. This is where my spy cave is. It was set up and secured to report to base. My goal for this job was to retrieve the prototype intact, get it to them and advise the players who knew about it. If I needed to take out the players who stopped me, so be it.

Just do it quietly, Hawk. No mess. No trace. We're counting on you.

The mission was off the grid as the British government had formed a small team in 1998 to build the prototype. Only this highly classified unit knew about it. It was a weapon of espionage to be employed on a needed basis against other countries. The head of SIS wanted to keep it under wraps, naturally. It would cause bedlam if the world found out. A few years back, a leak in the department led to two members being charged with treason. After that incident, those members disappeared off the face of the earth. They weren't taking any chances this time. That's why I was hired. I was off the grid and rogue, just the way I liked it. My tribe was warriors and so was I.

Every now and then I would take a residential gig - a member of regular society, but I didn't treat this like a standard assassin would. I had to know who the mark was and what the crime was. If I deemed it to be social justice - as I did with this case, then I assisted with the job. A delicate tightrope of moral code, but my elders taught me different laws. I saw it as maintaining the karmic balance of the planet. Sara, my protégé, would prefer justice was handled above board, but me? I played in the grey area. I would serve it up according to my ancestors' ancient laws. *Who cared that they showed up with a few broken fingers in court?* Elliot deserved to be exposed. Hiding behind his dirty drug money with his high society bloodlines.

Evana's cherry-red nails surfaced in my mind. They used to claw into my back during moments of passion. I used to be fond of that memory, but now it crushed me from the inside out. The only way out I could see was to erase Evana from my memory or win her back. I didn't know which way to go yet. My heart was confused, jumbled into too many compartments. One part was locked and closed off, another wanted to run to her and tell her the bold truth of who I was. The third wanted detachment so I could shield her. The fourth truly loved her and wanted to be by her side forever more. The trouble was reconciling all four. I didn't have time to consult the Chief directly. He didn't accept phone line communications. He was a person you had to visit directly. He would know what to do. I decided I would call on him through the dream portal. I could ask for his guidance and wisdom in this situation.

Currently my mind was on poisoning Elliot. Water hemlock ought to do the trick. The plant caused convulsions and foaming at the mouth. It would be a joy to watch his face. Particularly when the realization hit that he wasn't eating celery after all. On assignment in Sierra Leone, poison was the weapon of choice for the mark. He obtained highly classified information from the British government and was using it for extortion.

My mind kept flip-flopping between the case and Evana. I wasn't the *"if I can't have her, no-one can type of guy,"* but I was starting to feel that energy creeping into my soul. I refused to let it take me over. I just had to keep Sara off my scent for a minute longer. She had a way of prying information out of people at times and would be suspect if I continued asking about Evana.

14

SARA

♟

I had been chipping away all night trying to piece this case together. I wanted to nail Robert. *No, no, not like that*. Earlier on, admittedly – but not now. That attraction had been replaced with silent rage. My mindset of retribution for a just cause was back in its rightful place. A sobering reality check when you learn the man you're lusting after killed his wife's father, replacing him as a joke by marrying his daughter. *Sick fucking bastard*.

The case was now even more complex. I was working on a safe house situation for Evana. If Robert knew that Evana overheard the conversation, she would be a dead Vogue supermodel –and that wasn't happening on my watch. Pins, photographs, articles, police reports with connections covered my kitchen table. Along with a ham and cheese croissant from the local coffee shop. They sold the best ones. Croissants that melted in your mouth with cheese oozing out. Great case food and fuel for the brain.

Some things were missing about this case, and they weren't adding up. New discoveries. *What the hell was Clope and his sidekick goon doing at a schoolyard picking up a school kid for ten minutes, and riding him around the block? Did he have a school kid doing drug rounds now? Was he recruiting them younger? Or had he always been doing this?* I sensed there was an extra element to this case that would open Michael Sawyer's death.

So that's just what I did.

I wanted to go talk to this kid at the school. I figured I would stop by around lunch time and just scout out the place. Ask some questions about classes, sniff out the scene. I was parked fifteen meters away from the school in my blue zippy Honda. Out of my peripheral, I spotted an all-black truck, looked like a kitted-out Dodge Ram with tinted windows. I squinted, trying to get a glimpse at who was in the truck. I was busy twisting in my seat to gain better sight. All the while trying not to look suspicious. I scrunched down a little, so I wasn't visible. I didn't even know if it was anything at this point, but the way the truck rolled up I knew there was a strong likelihood that something was about to go down.

Brainwork was kicking in. All money launderers seemed to have a fall guy. You know: a guy who did all the dirty work while they stayed unstained. Fit the theme with Robert, allegedly cleaning his money through his companies. I said 'allegedly' because it wasn't proven in a court of law. Hawk told me this. He had street sources that worked closely with Robert and signed NDAs not to talk. My client worked with Elliot previously and gave me a document as proof. This backed up the claim. That agreement didn't stop them from squawking, according to Hawk. All that's done in the dark eventually came to light.

Large bags of money were dropped off on certain dates to particular warehouses. Codes were sent to his street crew for the drop offs. The burner phones they held were replaced every four weeks. It was a tight run operation that ran 24/7. Even for a criminal mastermind like Elliot. *I would find out.* I was ruminating on the dirty cop scene. If worse came to worst and no-one could be trusted, I would leak records to the press and hit him from a reputation standpoint. He wasn't going to win this. *Not anymore.*

I saw them drag the kid into the back of the car. He looked all of fifteen and scared as hell. *What could they possibly want with this kid? How did it fit in the picture?* Holy shit. I had my camera on standby and I managed to get off a round of six quick rapid-fire shots. I figured I had to get these pics to Hawk as soon as possible. Hawk had a Batcave, which he never invited me to – that was another story. I figured he had his reasons, and they usually were very good ones. Hawk could pick up the tiniest of megapixels with his equipment and locate places. I was hoping he could give me a solid ID on the second goon. I had a direct link from my camera to email, so I sent the photos to Hawk.

Hey, new info. Can you ID the kid for me? Can you get a read on the other goon with Clope? Sara.

Not even two minutes later:

Apologies for delay. ID already secured. Kid is Dean Noble. Mathematical genius. Top of his class off to Harvard. I should have told you earlier. Explain everything when I see you.

Damn you Hawk! Holding information back from me. I had stumbled onto something he was reluctant to get me involved in. This would make me start sniffing around a little more. *He had to tell me now.* I put two and two together quickly, realizing that this might be the missing link to Michael Sawyer I was searching for.

Fifteen minutes later, and the goons brought the kid back. I watched him being pushed out of the truck. He limped his way back onto the school grounds with a bloody nose.

Lunchtime. My eyes were blurry from staring at the same information too long. Turns out Michael Sawyer was an avid gamer and did a lot of coding at Mescon Technologies. He had links to government files. I was convinced he had a link to the Elliots. He was possibly working for them. I decided to take a walk. Might be time for another visit to the coffee shop for the second coffee drip. *Or maybe a permanent insert of a drip would work.* Lately I had been drinking too much of it. On my Vogue days off, I toned down to my regular dress code. Back to investigator mode. I was in my comfy pair of blue jeans and a white tee with my favorite Converse sneakers. My red jacket. I felt like I needed it at this point. No one from Robert's world would dare enter this neighborhood. It was too... How do I put it... "regular" for them. On this day, however, my Spidey senses were up. I had a distinct feeling of being followed.

Left corner of my eye, red car, slow tail. I put my hand on my right back pocket. It wasn't visible from the outside world, but I was tucked and strapped. The heat was on in this case, so I was taking no chances. My gun was registered; a good old Smith & Wesson. The car looked familiar. I turned to view a sleek candy red sports Porsche with a beaming Robert at the wheel. My heart started to pulsate so much it made my shirt vibrate from the beat of it. My head throbbed at the same time. Robert was dressed in a blue linen shirt. A few buttons were open as always. Polished hair slicked to the side and gleaming white teeth. *Ugh.* He slinked his ride up to the sidewalk and parked. My face radiated dismay and disgust. Internally I knew he'd caught onto me. *How else could he find me?* I was out in the open, so there was nothing he would do to touch me. Maybe a scare tactic or two. I wanted to see the game he was executing. I watched his movements as he exited the car. Scanned him. He wasn't reaching for anything. My insides eased a little.

"Oh, Sara, baby... You don't look too happy to see me. This is a different look for you. The red jacket. Suits you. I like it," Elliot observed, his voice like butter making me want to melt. Robert stepped in time with my walk. He was side by side with me.

Calm. Imagine an ocean of calm. I meditated from time to time, so I was trying to reach into my shallow closet of mindfulness to find some comfort. *Screw it. Not working.*

"Slumming today, Robert?" Shots were fired.

"If I get to see your pretty face, it's never slumming." He countered with silky smoothness. I surveyed the perimeters... plenty of people. Warm day. Witnesses everywhere. I lengthened my stride.

"Pouring on the charm as always, I see. What brings you to the neighborhood?" Calm, Sara. Play the game.

"Well, I have a good friend that lives on Grant Terrace. Such a beautiful place here. Don't you think, Sara?"

Dread dropped into my chest like a dead weight. Grant Terrace was the street my mother lived on. I would protect my mother at all costs. She never wanted me to become a P.I. Eventually she got used to it, though.

"I wish you could pick another job. It's way too dangerous. I couldn't live if anything happened to you." The dramatics were a constant with my mother. She poured it on when she needed to.

"Mom, I have back up and this is what I want to do. I'll be fine." I reassured her as much as possible, but she still fretted.

My teeth started to grind. *Oh, so you wanna play.* I gave my best poker face. *He knew.* I would have to outsmart this guy.

"How come I've never seen you around the area then? I'm sure I would have remembered a schmuck like you hanging around." My sarcasm levels were on high and I wanted it to cut straight through him. Robert let out an evil laugh that was irksome.

"Schmuck? We name calling now? What changed between us?" Stagnant silence.

"You stalking me brought on the change," I shot back.

"So, listen - have you thought any more about the job proposal of mine? I really could use some help in the office. There's a great coffee spot around here … Justine's. You know it? We could have a chat about it. I could run you through the job details and spend some time." I scanned my brain for a result. My mind computer was running separate wires - one to my vagina and the other to the short circuit in my skull. Both were giving me a shaky print out. The great thing was Elliot had no idea about my favorite coffee spot. I wouldn't have to change venues. Today I happened to be headed to Justine's because it was closer. I could get back to work faster. In and out is what I planned.

"Ok," I replied. My detective cap was on. We were a few short steps from the coffee shop at this point. He opened the door for me. I caught his lethal scent, treacherous lust lingered in the air. I willed myself to keep stabilized.

We slid into an empty booth. By all appearances, it was a regular day with regular people minding their business on the street. Mom's with strollers, couples holding hands, an old lady walking her poodle. Except this wasn't regular. I was seated in front of a cold-blooded criminal talking fake business, threatening erotic tension swirling around us like an impending typhoon. Robert's cold blue eyes pierced mine; a stare-off. I refused to look away. It was almost as if he was employing telepathic mind control. Robert spoke first. He was wearing the same cologne from the party. The scent was affecting my senses. Hypnotizing me.

"Nice to see you, Sara." A smooth talker was facing me.

"Can't say I feel the same." Fire. Let that sit in your heart, Robert.

"Why the change between us? I thought we were getting along well?" His tone was of the teasing variety.

"I told you. The change happened when you thought it was okay to stalk me on my day off." I wanted to cut to the chase of the situation.

"You have the wrong idea. Like I said, I was in the area. I have a friend here. Must say it was a nice surprise." That Colgate grin. The waitress came with our coffee. She had fallen for his spell as well. I looked over at his coffee, it had a love heart etched into it. I rolled my eyes. Mine had a lackluster swirl. No love heart for me. He smiled up at the waitress and winked at her.

"Thank you, doll face. You deserve a tip." He handed her a fifty-dollar bill, slipping it into her front pocket, and whispered, "Don't tell your boss about this. It's our little secret. The tip's just for you." The girl, who appeared to be all of seventeen, blushed, her docile eyes opening wide. She was almost dripping saliva onto her black tennis shoes. *Ughh.* If only she knew the guy was a sadist.

I took a swallow of my coffee, both hands around the cup for comfort. I observed Robert's movements while he was talking to the waitress. He flicked his Rolex watch into position. It was a little loose on his wrist. Looked like he had lost a little weight. Those cheekbones were a little more pronounced. *Stress perhaps? Was it the deal or the recent murder of Michael Sawyer that had him twisted?* The waitress slipped back behind the counter and ran to the other girl, flapping her hands. They started giggling together in unison.

"You see, Sara. A little extra money to line your pockets is always helpful. I come bearing gifts."

"I'm not looking for extra funds. Why don't you tell me what you're here for, Robert?" Straight talk, because this prick decided it was okay to stalk me. The irony is, I was stalking him. If only he could see my kitchen.

"Ok, so look - I need a new assistant because mine is leaving in two weeks. Have you considered my offer?" I opened my mouth to react. Leaving in two weeks? That was a lie. *You're going to fire her in two weeks is more likely.* A loud megaphone in my mind was speaking to me.

"Before you say no, let's just enjoy a cup of coffee together, whadda ya say?" Oddly enough that didn't take so much convincing. I was happy with that. I wanted to lay the sword down a minute anyway. A soft guard at the door would be enough.

"Sounds good. What do you want to know?" My curiosity was piqued. If he knew about me, let's see how the chess pieces would line up.

"I wanna know why a pretty girl from Maywood who doesn't seem to care about fashion is now working for Vogue." I froze in my seat. He knew where I lived. Fuck. The guards brought out their shields and their weapons. And just like that I was back on high alert, like I never left. Bile started to rise in my throat. I pushed it back down. His frosty blues were sealed on me. I looked straight back at him. *Brain scan, where did he get his information?* Maurice had provided a serious cover for me at Vogue. This is information no one knew. Had he been tailing me this whole time? I guessed it wouldn't have been that hard to find my location. I was in the hot seat, and truth be told, deep down I liked it. Toying with hot coals and tossing them back into the fire.

"I'm not sure where you got your information." I laughed it off as best I could. Inside my intestines were churning. My body felt constricted like I was bound in thick ropes.

"My sources are pretty airtight, Sara." His eyes narrowed. It was as if he was peering into my soul, not letting up for even a minute. "Well I guess you better re-check your sources."

"Hmm... interesting... I'm not trying to pry into your personal business. If I want to hire you, I make it my place to learn about new potential employees. Shouldn't be a problem if you have nothing to hide." Eerie placidity washed over me; Elliot had this effect on me.

"I haven't agreed to work with you, Robert. Plus, people change careers all the time. The job you want me to do sounds extremely boring and tedious. There's no way I want to be your errand girl."

Robert's face expanded with a sleek smile. "No, no. You

could be my party host, private jets, endless holidays, great fashion and gala events. Not appealing?" He gulped his coffee down.

"Hell no. I can't be bought." I snorted at his list of meaningless items. He was used to dangling the carrot to a different type of woman. I was not interested.

"So, how did you come to be in fashion? You don't really strike me as being that superficial. You seem to be a woman of substance." Here's where bluff stations came in... and why did he assume fashion was shallow?

"It's more about the movement, colors of the materials that I really love and all the great people you get to meet." That sounded lame as hell. Something Maurice said to me. My awkwardness was out in the open. Let me tuck it back in.

Robert smirked. "There is a dark side to fashion that's for sure. As you've seen."

"Robert, you have outlandish parties with drugs everywhere. Hollywood types. Yet, you come from a bloodline of old tycoons and business minds. Why the switch up?" You're trying to make me uncomfortable; I'm going to make you squirm, too, *bitch*.

"I love a party – that's for sure. So do my clients. It's just for show. A way to entertain, impress, and keep the effervescence flowing. You don't seem to mind. You're at every party I host lately. Need I remind you that anything that happens at my house remains confidential?"

"I wasn't aware you were watching me." Sidestepping the threat with a counter of my own. I twiddled my thumbs around my coffee cup, averting my eyes from his gaze to check my surroundings for a moment. No goons of Robert that I could see. So, this was a solo visit from him.

"Oh yes, you were. You're aware of my presence – that's for sure. I know you can feel the electricity between us. Stop trying to avoid it. Face it head on." I swear I saw Elliot's eyes change color. Almost like a turquoise tropical pool of tranquility. I wriggled in my seat. He knew how to apply pressure, that was for sure. Elliot touched my forearm from across the diner booth. I recoiled and pulled my hand back quickly, but not before the energy transfer of sensuality made its way to me.

"Sara." This guy was a maestro. "I just want to spend some time with you, to be real. But I am a professional. I could really use your help in the office. I'm swamped in a mountain of paperwork." A strange conundrum was occurring. A moment of actual truth from Robert. It felt like it could be. Or was he playing with my mind?

"I feel this is inappropriate, Robert. You are a married man. Or did you forget?" I heard my voice outside of it. I sounded so formal and stiff.

"Soon to not be married."

I sat my coffee cup down. Shock hit my system. "Are you separating from Evana?"

"We haven't been good for a long time. Don't say anything to her. You're the first person I'm confiding in with this information." He looked down at his coffee and cleared his throat. I saw his Adam's apple bob up and down. As if something was stuck there. He was finding this hard to discuss. A moment of truth. This part I could believe.

I drew back in my seat. A quick summation without a hint of recognition on my face. Didn't want to give it away that I knew. *Did he know what Evana overheard? What was his plan*? I had to work carefully with him, to decode the hints, keep Evana safe and solve this case. I had Hawk in my back pocket. Ultimately, everything was going to turn out for the best.

Which led me back to the chopped-up body parts in the Hudson river that he was linked to. If I worked for him, I could work on linking a paper trail. Find out his links to Mescon Technologies. Time to go fishing.

"So, Robert... What do you do in your down time?"

"I really like to relax. Kick back. See new places. Nothing out of the ordinary."

"Ok, Ok. Personally, I like video games."

"Video games? You do? Well, there you go." He had no idea where I was headed with this. The confusion on his face told me that.

"Yeh, I like Mortal Kombat. I enjoy technology. So much of it out there. Really is the wave of the future."

"That I agree with. I have a few technology stocks and bonds and they're moving fast." Getting warmer. I pretended to lean in and be interested.

"Wow. Must be doing well, then. Drone technology seems to be the next big thing for the armed forces. Might be something to look into, huh?" A shift. Subtle enough that I saw his change in demeanor. His eyes moved away from me for the first time since we sat down. Clenched jaw. I saw it ripple. Forearm twitching. He was involved in something high-tech. *I sensed it.*

You see, one strand leads to the next. A slow reveal occurs. All I had to do was feed this man's ego. Elliot couldn't help but boast to me about his stocks.

"Might be the thing. Who knows?" Robert shrugged. He was trying to downplay his distress.

Pandora's box had been opened and there was no closing the lid. I had enough to report back to my client. Next, it was time to pay Michael Sawyer's mother a visit. Hard to do since Elliot knew where I lived now. Things just got a little tricky.

My game plan was to see Elliot behind bars for a substantial amount of time. I would either have to penetrate Robert's network and dig deeper or have the man confess somehow, someway. That would be a dangerous game to play. Becoming Elliot's lover, gaining his trust and having him pillow talk about his past indiscretions. Thought had crossed my mind. That kind of game I wasn't sure I was equipped for... and really, was it worth it?

I mean, he did reveal his secret about Evana's father on the wire. *But to have him slip again?* No, I had to catch Robert in another way. Hit him right between the eyes.

On the money train. To strip away his business, to expose his money laundering, to expose the drug crime syndicate which was running rampant across Hollywood. To expose the old money train and make sure it stuck in court for a long time. No doubt Elliot would have a string of serious attorneys if he was caught. That wouldn't stop me. I had the endurance to see it through. This was only the initiation of it all.

Intel for the case was building solidly, especially with Hawk along for the ride. *The problem was how much time did I have?* I was seriously attracted to this man and the imp side of me was really loving it. A side of me never shown, only in my fantasies. I was powerless to it. My mind resisted, but my body persisted with its hungry urges. It was refusing to play ball no matter how I tried. Let the attraction be there, I figured. Let it sit. Until I figured out what the hell to do with it.

"Earth to Sara." I had drifted off away from the situation at hand. I was sifting through the pieces together in my fog-covered brain.

"I'm here, but I really don't know why you're telling me this. I mean, I barely know you, and Evana is a colleague and a friend of mine."

"Forget her for a minute. I'm telling you because I know you feel what I feel." Robert's tone contained sincerity. *Did he mean what he was saying? This guy was good.*

"I don't see that we have much in common, Robert. I really don't."

"I think we have a lot more in common than you think. Who do you think got Evana a foot in the door at Vogue? She was doing chump modeling up until I put her on." Robert studied my face intently for acknowledgement.

"Hmm, I see. Still doesn't tell me what we have in

common." My lips were dry. I was having a hard time staying neutral.

"Attraction, stimulating conversation, you're a go getter; classy and savvy. I like that." Robert leaned in with a hushed tone.

"Don't see how that's enough." *Liar, liar pants on fire!!* I wanted to jump across the table and have him take me in his arms. To feel those sexy lips on mine, if only for a while. To say I tasted danger and won. *Was I desperate?* Surely there was a better way for me to get my kicks in life. But that wasn't the appearance given, thank God. I was tame at the table and presented as a lady. I tried not to let him see that he had affected all my senses in such a way that I could barely breathe for fear I would be found out.

Sara, the lover of criminals! Sara, the private detective that took a walk on the dark side. Never to return from the abyss of her downfall. Escaped to Cabo, a fugitive on the loose! That's what the headline would read.

"Oh, it's plenty," he paused fixing his gaze on me. "Your body is saying everything I need to know right now." The corner of his lips curled up into a mysterious smile. His boyish good looks mixed with a three o'clock shadow was enticing indeed. My face was flushed with heat the moment he said it. I was certain my cheeks were beetroot red. Robert appeared to be amused, so it must have been true.

"Sara, have a think about my offer. Let me know by tomorrow. Sleep on it. Hell, I would much rather you would sleep with me, but we can get to that." Elliot slid a napkin with a price across it and I knew it had a lot of zeros attached to it. I lost sound. I stared at the napkin, then at him. *Shit.*

"I will get back to you, Robert, I don't know if it will be by tomorrow. Enjoy your stay in the area." Holy shit – that was a lot of money. But the strings attached would far outweigh the pleasures. That was a given. I see why women found him hard to resist. I saw the allure now. Experienced it firsthand.

"It's always a pleasure when I see you, Sara," the words slid like satin off his well-made lips. Inside I felt my insides flip flop. Robert got up from the booth, dropped a fifty on the table and left. I watched him as I took a controlled sip of my coffee. If anyone looked closer, they could see the tremor in my fingers. I waited briefly to check if he would look back. He didn't. Time to call in the cavalry. I picked up my phone to call Hawk.

The game was on and now I was caught up in it.

♟

SHE WAS SHAKY, on edge. I wanted her to know that I was aware of who she was. The drop was scheduled on June 15th and nothing could alter that. I wanted to get her off the scent, though. At the same time, Evana had to go. She was a liability.

Much to do, much to do.

All before an investor meeting at twelve. A man's work is never done. I hadn't lied to Sara – just omitted. *I did want her.* I was swamped with paperwork in the office. *I did have feelings for her.* She was smart. She would figure out that I knew who she was. I was five steps ahead of her, though. But hey, Sara, let's play for a while. *All's fair in love and war, right?* If I could just get her under my clutches, that's when things would really start to gain momentum.

♟

TWO DAYS LATER, I was staring at my wall of investigation in my apartment. Figuring out the missing jigsaw pieces. I found out Michael Sawyer's mother didn't live in New York anymore; she was in Kansas. I tried calling a list of numbers, but none of them were hits. I was going to see if Hawk could speed up the process.

Case recap: A pissed off client avenging the death of his son, a smooth playboy criminal who I had the hots for, a supermodel with death impending, an unreachable assassin, a geeky prototype maker, a raspy-voiced goon, and now an insidious game of cat and mouse. All of it was enough to send a woman like me looney.

When I tuned into the radio surveillance, the conversations on the airwaves talked of date changes. See-sawing conversations between Elliot and Clope. There was talk of bringing forward the date of the drop. Seemed strange they would talk so openly on the wire. Wasn't consistent from what I heard from them. They spoke more of where to meet rather than the longer conversations they were having the last couple of days. Not so much code. It really didn't sit well in my gut. Something felt off, it seemed a li'l too easy flow for my liking.

Yeah, Clope, you ready to make the drop? How about we move this forward? And what about a change to the warehouse? Let's say down near Pier 18 just behind the old donut factory.

"Ah, yeh, I know the one boss. It's a shame they closed down. They used to do the best apple jelly donuts in the city." No wonder Clope resembled a doughnut. Lucky his victims were usually up close because if it involved a foot chase Clope wasn't your guy. Detective humor.

Elliot responded, "I know, but now there will be donuts of another kind in production." Wicked laughter ensued.

Things weren't kosher. And how did this kid come into the equation? I made a mental note to catch the kid before school tomorrow and buy *him* a donut. All the talk of donuts made me hungry. *Seriously.* Meanwhile, my plan was to move Evana from Elliot's house. So far, I thought it best to use her work. A shoot in Mexico, somewhere offshore. That would keep her safe temporarily until another solution came together.

15

SARA

♟

The boy heaved a blue backpack slumped over one shoulder. White converse sneakers, plaid shirt, part schoolboy prep in style. One of those asymmetrical haircuts that nerdy emo teenagers were sporting these days. God knows why. He kept flicking it out of his eye, with a head toss that resembled a twitch gone wrong. Dean looked troubled as he slunk across the school grounds. He kept glancing over his shoulder, like he was waiting for someone to come grab him. I was parked across the road from the school. *If I was quick, I could catch him.* I jumped out of my Honda and proceeded with a quick stride towards the oval. I caught up to him within twenty meters, he turned in defense with his palms up.

"Leave me alone! I don't know anything." His eyes gave way to terror. Upon a closer look I saw the kid had a ring around the bottom of his eye like someone socked him a right hook. *Had he been hit for not delivering something?*

"Wait! I'm not going to hurt you!" I had my palms up in

passiveness. By now I had broken into a slow jog to keep up with him.

"Hey! I'm a detective and I want to help you!" I called out to him.

"I can't. They said they're going to kill me! Please! I just want to go to class." The voice of a very scared teenager came back at me.

"Who's going to kill you?" I inquired. "Just tell me what you're involved in and I can make sure to get you some help. I'm here to help. It's ok." I held up my hands to show I had no weapons and that he was safe. I understood his trepidation. This had to be his worst nightmare come to life.

"Let me show you my detective's license." He slowed in pace; he was becoming a little more open to the idea.

"That doesn't mean anything. They can be forged." He side-eyed me and kept walking ahead, hitching his bag as he went.

"Trust me, ok?" I pleaded. He stopped and faced me.

"I thought it was a simple hack job and I don't want to go to jail. They wanted me to help them develop an X- ray vision satellite, so they can sell it on the black market and make millions." The kid was incredibly nervous and spilled all the beans. I hoped he hadn't told anybody else.

"Who are they?" I needed facts to stand on.

"Some fat guy with a weird accent, plus some other bald guy." Reminded me of Ren and Stimpy. The kid still had his sense of humor. Which was unheard of, given his position. Maybe death threats brought out his comedic streak.

"Have you completed the job for them? And have you told anybody else about it?"

"No and no. There's some glitches with it, hence the black eye, I guess." He rubbed his eye socket that was partially covered by his emo haircut.

"I have two more days to finish it. Gracious of them.

Otherwise they said they would kill my Mom." The kid's nose was running. He looked like a wildebeest that had been caged for months. I grabbed my tape recorder from my bag when the kid ducked down behind the tree. He pointed out towards the school courtyard which was visible from the oval. Robert was playing a game. June 15th was two days away. *Why were they waiting so late? Wouldn't they want the device before the drop?*

"There's one of the guys now! *OMG – dead meat.*" I put my hand on my gun holster. The guy in question was Clope. He was indeed Robert's goon. He was looking especially goonish dressed in all black. He was scanning the schoolyard for him. The school bell rang out for first class. Clope appeared angry at the noise, like he missed his moment. He was prowling now, his ugly face desperate for answers. I grabbed the kid by the back of the shirt as instincts kicked in. I told him to bob down further. I meant business today. I knew my red jacket would come in handy.

"Stay down and don't move." My voice held strength and firmness. We were crouched behind a big oak tree which reached into the schoolyard about ten meters away. Clope was closing the gap. Dean shook in fear next to me. I kept a steadfast grip on his shoulder to settle him. Clope couldn't seem to see what he was looking for. He looked out in our direction, and seemingly satisfied he saw nothing, moved towards the exit of the school yard. He drove off in a black Jeep Cherokee.

"Close call, huh kid?" The kid stepped out from behind the tree and doubled over.

It appeared he had pissed himself. A big ol' wet patch in the crotch area was evidence of this.

16

SARA

♟

"**O**k let's get you cleaned up." Poor kid. I felt for him. He was really going through it.

Dean's face was covered in scarlet red. He stammered. "Th-th-that was a close call. I gott-ttta go to the bathroom. I think I peed myself." I stared at the kid in pity. Was understandable, really. I would have peed myself, too, if killers came to my school talking about eliminating my family.

"Sure thing, I'll be waiting outside. Don't worry – you're safe now." I sucked in a low sigh. This case was getting out of hand. Time for order to be restored. So many complications, so many woven pieces that needed to be stitched together just right to bring the fabric of the case together.

"How do you know they won't come back?" Dean squinted at me in terror.

"Well, we don't, but just like I got you out of trouble then, I will again. We can figure out a plan together." I threw the kid a reassuring smile that even I didn't believe at this point. I waited outside the toilet block. The kid emerged ten minutes later with a slightly damp face and wet hair, looking perplexed and frightened at the same time.

"Let's find somewhere we can talk. Do you have class right now?" I didn't want him to lose his scholarship on top of all this.

"Ahh no, I gotta break between mathematical computing and crypto." He seemed a little calmer, a few tendrils of his hair were slicked to his face. Looked like he splashed some water on it. I stole a peek at his crotch area. The area was dry but had a distinctive ring around it and the air smelt a little like pee combined with spray deodorant.

"What's crypto?"

"Oh, it's short for cryptography." *Of course.* I had no freaking idea what kind of class that was, but it sounded hella smart. I dropped my sunglasses off my nose. This kid looked all of five feet tall and was about the size of a toothpick. He squinted back at me with expectancy.

"What? You've never heard of it?"

"No, can't say I have, but I'm willing to learn if it's gonna catch these bad guys. Tell me what they got you working on more specifically."

We found a bench out the back of the cafeteria. A bunch of college kids were chatting and laughing with their friends, others were scurrying off like squirrels to classes they were late for. I brought the kid a coffee. I put it down in front of him.

"Ok. Spill."

"Well at first I thought it was just restoring the proto-type. The purpose of it is to search large databases and retrieve key information components by satellite login. Inclusive of this the x-ray component is to gain video and audio footage from the surrounding environment. The footage that can be seen is super sharp and can pick up microscopic sound. It's like surround sound only twenty hundred times better. Makes you feel like you're right in it.

It's panoramic, too. You can swivel around the room or space you're in." The kid really knew his shit. If this wasn't a super important case, I would sit down and pick his brain. His eyes started to light up and his face turned up in a smile. This was his path in life. I could tell. Too bad the assignment was for bad guys. He was destined to do some extraordinary things in life.

"So, what you're telling me in layman's terms is that this is a spy machine?" The decibels of my voice went up a notch.

"Well yeah, but it's way more advanced. This is not Google Earth I'm talking about. I mean this puppy can pick up clear-cut audio from miles away. It can decipher and decode the voices on-screen with hella precision. It traces the names of the people talking, gives addresses, times, dates and coordinates. There's nothing like it in the world," he spoke confidently. Dean spread his arms out, his excitement couldn't be tempered. I sipped my coffee and waited for him to continue.

"No wonder they want to keep it a secret. This thing could ruin people. I plan on testing it on this girl I like. I want to see if she's talking about me. I wanted to ask her to the school dance." I rolled my eyes at the boy. Ok, he might have been a genius, but he was still a hopeless boy who was clueless about the opposite sex.

"Better off just asking her to go with you." The kid looked across at me, wide-eyed.

"Think she'd wanna go with me?" he asked nervously. This kid was worrying about a school dance, but if he didn't deliver to these goons, he might be dancing underground. I suppose he wanted to have a light at the end of the tunnel.

"Of course, why wouldn't she? You're smart and a good-looking kid," I said with encouragement.

"Thanks." The kid started blushing. We both took a moment to sit with things. Dean sipped his coffee. I was busy letting my brain propel me to the next important questions.

"Ok, did they have you looking at any specific locations?" I asked.

"Ah yeah, they had me looking at specific countries." Bingo.

"What countries did they have you looking at?"

"Czech Republic, London, Russia, and United States: Washington and Boston," Dean confirmed with clarity.

"Ok, did they say they would be contacting you soon?" I asked with anxiety sitting in the pit of my stomach.

"Ah yeah, they have me on a schedule. I have to report back to them tonight. They said they're taking me somewhere for a meeting." This sounded like a stupid plan from Elliot's perspective. I mean this kid was out in the open! Why hadn't they kidnapped him? Would have been easier. He could have been working around the clock on the prototype. Weren't they concerned that the kid would tell?

"Are you able to do what they want you to do?"

"Yes, I can. But I'm having trouble cracking this last component of the coding and making it work together. I am getting a fuzzy picture from these locations and can't quite get it clear. It's pretty good, though. I've improved on the prototype, so it could work." *For sure they planned to kill this kid.* He was a database of information. No way would they let him go. He didn't know that, though. Another one I had to protect. This whole case was like a malignant spider's web, intricately weaved by the grandmaster, Elliot. Therefore, Michael Sawyer got chopped up. This is why his body was found floating in the Hudson river. This was it. I just had to prove it and I would be home free.

"Uh-huh. Do they pat you down when they meet up with you?"

"Yes. I have to do a strip search. It's embarrassing. I gotta say this is not the most pleasant experience I have had as a kid." Damn. I couldn't put a wire on him.

"I can imagine. Do they do anything to you? Please tell me they don't." I laid my hand on top of his.

"No. They just check quickly and ask me to put my clothes back on."

"You didn't try and tell your family?" Dean's eyes were full of sadness as he answered.

"No, they said they would know if I did and stab me in the night. I can't sleep some nights." None of this was adding up. Wouldn't his parents suspect if he was in his bedroom all the time?

"How could you work on this? Especially when your parents are home?" The kid blew out a sigh that shifted his hair from his eye. The one they had punched him in.

"My parents work a lot. Both. They really don't notice the things I do. They just want me to go to Harvard and make them rich, so they can stop working." Exploitation. I felt the rage coursing through my system. Right under their nose. Made me sick.

"What about your eye?"

Dean shrugged. "Eh, I told them it was from gym class and that I got in a fight. First time my dad gave me a pat on the back. He was proud. He always called me a sissy before that." I breathed out to the sky; this was getting worse. Some people didn't deserve to have children.

"It's going to be ok. I'm going to make sure you're ok. I promise." I spoke with tenderness to Dean. I wanted him to know he at least had me in his corner.

"I'm so scared. These guys are big. I'm just a kid. Please help me." The kid's bottom lip started to quiver and tears banked up in his eyes. His nose started to run profusely. The kid was all messed up. The act of false bravado had dropped.

"I don't want anything to happen to my Moms."

"We are going to catch these guys. Here's what I need you to do..."

17

ELLIOT

T hose sweet lips tasted like honey. *Sara Clemens*. I was going to make her mine one way or another. I vowed to have her, but first... the pressing matter of eliminating my current wifey. A little downtown get together with Clope would fix that. Set the wheels in motion. I can't say I felt too much remorse about Evana's father. Just one of those irritating business situations. He impended my progress, so I had to get rid of him. I gave him a window of grace, but the old man was too stubborn for that. He left me no choice. Thwarting my plans for this major deal was not something I would've let happen. *I run this town.* NYC is mine. I had everything set up just how I wanted it. I knew where Clemens lived. I would let her sweat that a little. Give her some breathing space to gather herself. Make her think I didn't know everything yet. I saw how she froze in her seat when I told her I knew she wasn't a Vogue girl. I saw her faltering movements. The correction. I had eyes all over the city, though. Nothing escaped me.

Evana, on the other hand, was starting to grate at me. If

she overheard the conversation like I think she did, then who knows what she would come up with. She caught me slipping. Normally, my team talked in code. That night, I messed up. *Time to tighten up.* This deal had to go through; it would take my operation to the next level of non-fuckery. I could open a new distribution network and branch out. A little more risk, but monumental gain. Possibly close a quarter of drug operations and open up in arms dealing. Satellites. Higher stakes. More to think about, but it could be done. I liked to live on the edge. Surpass what my father did. I was sick and tired of living in his shadow. I would have to call a meeting with the team; the changing of the guard was coming. I was getting tired of dealing with these low-level street fucks. Too many chinks in the armor of late. A couple of my best guys were getting high off their own supply. I couldn't use them. I needed pure money-hungry sharks in place. Avery was one I could take with me. He was making me a fistful of additional income.

The chess game with Sara was becoming more calculated. Only thing is it didn't seem to feel so much like a game anymore. Intense feelings were creeping in, haunting my dreams. Her mystique, her awkwardness. I found it endearing. The boldness she possessed to challenge me. *What made her chase these criminals? Could she live on the wild side with me?* Those lips. The thunderbolt of emotion ripping through me when I consumed her lips. My dick grew hard when I left the café. I had to readjust myself. She didn't pull away either. The demure softness of her eyes had a sedative effect. I was the one that had to leave from the door. I felt too much in that kiss. A soft spot was building in my heart, shrinking my killer instinct. No way in hell would I let this go.

"Clope. Yeah. 45. Meet you there. Get the crew together. We have work to do."

18

HAWK

♟

I hit the pavement like I always did at the crack of dawn, before the world rose. The exercise rewound me back to my army days, when the sergeant would pound on our bunk beds at three a.m. He would have us run eight miles blindfolded. A wry smile came over my face; I was the leader of the pack on that one.

Valiant men of strength and honor existed amongst my legion. I missed those guys. Every couple of years if we could, we got together to reminisce over old times. Most of the crew were based on the East Coast of the United States. How that happened I would never know. We were not so far from one another. Brothers in arms. Never failed to take me back to those nostalgic moments. That was the training ground of the man who I'd become: Hawk.

My headphones were buckled in and I was cloaked in a black hoodie. Eye of the Tiger pulsating through my earbuds. Adrenaline streamed through my system. I lived for the thrill of taking down criminals like Elliot. Watching Elliot corner Sara at the coffee shop made me realize his deception toolkit ran deep. I was shaking my head as I saw Sara being yanked onto Elliot's chessboard.

I slammed my fists on the steering wheel as I sat across the road. I saw Sara reciprocate the kiss. *I warned her about the guy, and what does she do?* She falls for the guy. I thought of Sara as one of my field operatives, and you never leave a woman or man down. Elliot was starting to cloud her better judgment. I had to put the nail in the coffin on this one, help her.

Turns out the nerdy kid- Dean Noble – was ever so close. This emo-looking kid stood on the precipice of cracking a code that could destroy the world. I knew Elliot's ego had overtaken him, otherwise he would have this kid under his grip. Why would you give the kid the prototype and let him work on it freely? So, my only answer was that he was cocky. He thought nobody knew. Shame on you, Elliot. Leaving your backdoor open. The Secret Intelligence Service wanted the prototype contraband and I was instructed to steal it back immediately. I had to talk my superiors off the ledge on that one.

Get us the prototype immediately. No ifs, ands, or buts. It's your ass on the line, Hawk.

Sit tight. Have I ever not delivered? I have it in hand. Wait for the play-out. The takedown is bigger than you think.

You better. The world is riding on your back. You know the stakes. Need I remind you of the consequences?

I understand. I will deliver as promised.

Good. Report usual time.

I scraped by, getting my way. If I didn't, I was going to take matters into my own hands and expose Elliot. Slowly grind him down over time. The drop was scheduled on June 15th, even though Elliot relayed on the wire as June 14th. His method of psychological games to confuse Sara. He found out she was a private investigator. How? I didn't know. But he knew, and that was the problem. Through research and my underground links in the spy game, I had a clearer list of dirty cops. McGarthy was one of them. I was waiting on a couple of confirmations from key sources on all the others.

Clope, the one that resembled a smushed up Mac truck, was en route with Elliot to a meeting. After their rendezvous, I planned on swinging by Sara's for our next steps. So far, Evana remained safe. I had her on high watch alert.

I was parked in a position with a high-power optic telescope. Crouched in a camouflage position. A dilapidated high rise infested with crackheads. Made sense, because of visibility and proximity to the meeting spot. Plus, no one would suspect me to be parked up here. Twelve p.m. Clope and Elliot were walking and talking at a snappy pace. Elliot's deep green trench coat flapping behind him. It was the fucking middle of summer. What was he wearing it for? Must have air con inside the building. Mr. Playboy and those black patent leather shoes. *Weirdo.* Clope strode beside him in a Boston-style henchmen coat. Both were talking in animation. They entered the side of a building. What looked to be an old meat warehouse. Elliot looked around nervously before he went in. Clope ushered him in. I had the location tapped. I checked for static in my ear and got ready for the download.

"Ok, you know the drill, let's run inventory."

"Ok, this one's gonna be fun, boss. I gotta tell ya. I'm looking forward to it." Sickly laugh from Clope. Then my wire cut out for some reason. *Fuck!* I reconnected the cables. Took me ninety seconds to get re-organized. Who knows what I missed? *I needed a time and date from them.* The next part of the puzzle. Otherwise, I would commune with my ancestors on this one. I would anyway, but if I could get the information now it would save time.

"Ok, so we got the time." Elliot was talking. Another two men entered from the side of the alley. *Oh shit.* Looked like a house meeting to check in with his crew.

"Avery, how's the West Side looking right now?"

"Third quarter and we up boss, 400. We looking good,"

Avery answered. Street dude. Up 400. 400 what exactly? 400,000 or $400? I suspected the former.

"Good, good." I heard Elliot slap him on the back and the faint clink of glasses. This was his clubhouse location. Or one of them, seemed.

"Let's make a toast to being up in all districts and the branching out of a new operation. I need you guys on your toes. This is higher stakes we're entering. Includes an extra $100k in all your pockets."

"That's wassup boss. We got your back." That money was small fry. Elliot was worth billions. Another voice spoke. One of the other guys that came late. I had an ID on the guy. I would run it through the system later. The conversation went on, more street codes, more distributors announcing numbers. Robert was checking in with his crew.

"So, Avery, I'm proud of you. You're killing it over there. If I up your shipment by three you got it?" Elliot enquired.

"Yeah, I got it. Easy. Summer parties are coming up. Few new millionaires in town," Avery responded casually. No locations were being mentioned, but he did say West.

"Great news. That's a wrap, crew. Any concerns, hit the burner and trash it." Elliot was wrapping things up.

Tables and chairs squeaked and shifted. A quick meeting – half an hour. The guy was good. Not too many guys in the operation... or were there more? Two guys fanned out and went their separate ways in two different vehicles. One got picked up in a black truck and the other in a black Chevy. What was it with criminals and black vehicles?

I shifted position slightly and heard my knee crack.

"Alright. Alright. Slight problem. Wifey." Elliot and Clope had stayed in the building. AG & Sons. The red lettering had faded away on the sign and the building wasn't a standout. You wouldn't even pay attention to it. I took note.

My ears were open and receptive. *This was what I was here for.* Elliot spoke. I was perched waiting, sweat dripping off the end of my nose. We were in the middle of summer in New York and my punk ass was wearing all black. The squat obviously had no air con or heating. Flies were buzzing and two dirty mattresses were behind me. One with a used needle sticking out from under it. *Sad*. The walls were stained a sickly mustard yellow color and it smelled faintly of piss in the building. I didn't have much time in the location before the druggies came back. I had given them $80 and a meal. I had to clear the area and set up. I knew they were probably out scoring right now. I sat tight. My knees were going to seize up if I didn't change position. That didn't matter. The sweat droplet fell off my nose. *Man, it was hot in this bitch.*

"So, timeline is up. We moving on it."

"I got the hitter, Boss." Squished-up face guy was talking. Clope.

"He's going to take her on a little ride. One she won't forget."

"Ok, good. Clope, I want, you know, nowhere near this thing. We had to clean up after you with...Sawyer. That wasn't supposed to happen." *There it was*. That nail. I had the tape. I just had to get it to Sara. *So Clope was the killer.* He had fucked up with the floating body parts in the river. Messy. Elliot had weak links in his team. He needed to get those egos in check. You're only as good as your weakest link, in my opinion.

"I hear you, Boss – that's my bad. He's clean, sharp and clinical. He'll get the job done. He's not called The Viper for nothing." Clope spoke with that frog in his throat again.

"Got a time on it?"

"No, that's not how the Viper works. He just lets you know when the job is done," Clope answered. "Protects you as the client and himself."

"Perfect," Elliot replied.

"So, you'll get the text?"

"Yup. My phone. You won't be implicated, boss," Clope

responded to his master. What made him so loyal? Was Clope not smart enough to know that Elliot could expose him at any time? Elliot must have something over Clope. Either that or Mac Truck Face matched his brain cells. Either way, Elliot was putting on a clinic right now. Anytime now, Evana could get picked up. I missed the ball on this one. My mind flashed with the vision I had. Ravens... the hogtie through her mouth. Time to exit.

I packed down with maximum efficiency and speed. I had about an hour before Clemens was due to the shoot with Evana. I know Evana was on a shoot location now. She had two today. I had to get a message to her. I sent it via an encoded number she wouldn't recognize.

You're in danger. I need you to follow my instructions. Trust me. I'm your guardian angel. She shot back like I knew she would.

Who the fuck is this? Is this a prank?

No. I'm trying to prevent your death. I know Robert killed your father. Follow Clemens.

Listen asshole I don't know who you are, but stay the hell away from me! I left it alone. She would follow. She would listen. Clemens would tell her. Robert, the sick bastard, sent that black rose – not me. A true piece of shit. A warning: the black rose symbolizes hatred, despair, and death.

I parked three streets away from Sara's apartment. Black t-shirt. Low olive-green cap. Black cargos. Black lightweight sneakers. Inconspicuous. My earphones were in. I broke into an easy stride run. I wanted people to think I was a normal civilian out for a jog. I slunk around the back door to Clemens's house.

"Hey, psst." I hissed and tapped with one knock. Sara checked out the window next to the back door, opening the door just a crack.

"Hey." She looked fraught. Like she'd been up all night. Still pretty. She kissed that clown. I knew she didn't bank on that happening. That's just what Elliot did. He was the Pied Piper of the opposite sex. He wielded a certain finessing power over females.

"So... Wanna tell me what the hell you were doing kissing the perp?" My anger spilled over. I wanted her to recognize the consequences.

"That wasn't me. It was him." Not too much to say about it. Her eyes searched the floor as if something important lay there. Her dignity, maybe.

"I'm about to head to the shoot." Sara's face held a clinical expression.

"You strapped?" I asked.

"Yep. Strapped. Smith and Wesson."

"Ok, like I taught you. Flick up and aim. Hold steady for the recoil if you need to fire." She breathed out a shaky sigh and cracked her neck, moving it side to side like a heavy-weight in the ring.

"Focus on keeping everything smooth. I will case the perimeter; run the shoot as usual. I got the names on most of the cops. I sent the list across. New blood is coming in the drug department. We can tip him off for the bust. Then straight to the airport for Evana. I got my guy waiting there."

"Ok. I'm ready." Sara spoke with determination. A grim look crossed her face. She had on her red leather jacket. "They changed the date. I feel like they're going to throw us off with the kidnapping. I've got a feeling they have a different date. Elliot knows about me."

"I know. I knew when he kissed you. He's playing with you now. The date is the same. June 15th. Stay the course." I peered at her; she shot me an astonished look.

"I know. I know. I'm solid." Shame was hidden in her voice for the kiss. I would let her off on that one. I knew what that experience was. To get caught up in a situation you can't get yourself out of. Hell, I was in one with Evana.

"Clemens, you're out of your depth on this one. The deal

is bigger than you think. If you have any remote feelings lurking for this dude, get rid of them now."

"I hear you." Her stare was blank. If Elliot had her heart, there would be no turning back for Sara.

"This is what we gotta do…"

19

SARA

The director insisted on low-level lighting for the next shoot. We were on our way out of New York at 2 p.m. in the afternoon. The theme for the shoot: a nature-inspired vibe for a major brand's new jungle print collection. The director, Sven Lankin, wanted the scene to be 'authentic and earthy.' Nine of us were packed in a white minibus heading to the outskirts of New Jersey. Norvin Green State Forest to be exact. I never knew the place existed before today. An expansive, rugged haven of pristine natural surroundings. A toll had been taken on Evana; her face appeared to be haggard from everything going on. Even within her dire emotional state, a twinkle of light existed. Some people were born with star power; Evana happened to be one of them. I squeezed her hand as soon as I saw her. We had agreed to keep everything as routine as possible so she could follow my instructions.

"What the fuck is going on?" she mumbled at me under her breath as we all tumbled into the minivan. I directed her to the back of the van where we could speak out of earshot. I envisioned being in her position. Her husband, the murderer, was now trying to kill her. I would want to run to the end of the earth and not return if I was her. Unfortunately, she picked one of the most powerful men in New York City. Not that easy to pull up your skirt and run from. Strategies had to be put in place first.

Before I left the house, I made sure I had my bullet-proof vest on. My Smith and Wesson Magnum revolver was firmly strapped in my waistband at the small of my back. Nice and tight to my body. Nobody knew I was packing heat. It was a precautionary measure and one I had never employed. I was skeptical of my own ability to fire. *I had six rounds in the barrel to fire.* What if I missed completely? After all, I would be trying to hit a moving target. That shit ain't easy. I had given Maurice the heads up to secure the location. He didn't ask questions. He said a security official was going to be standing guard when we got to the park. I wasn't so confident. My whole body was vibrating on high alert.

"You mean the text message?" I peered at her for the reaction. Her eyes nearly boggled out of her head. Hawk had sent her a warning message. *"You knew about it! Who the fuck is that? I couldn't trace the number back!"*

"Someone who has both of our best interests at heart. You're covered. Let's get through this jungle shoot and then you're on the plane to Mexico." My tone was businesslike; I wanted to instill confidence in the situation even though I knew nothing of the outcome. All I knew was that in working with Hawk we always ended up on our feet and alive.

The drop date remained the same, despite Elliot's games. Hawk got the tip-off from his own surveillance. In being the P.I. investigating the murder of Michael Sawyer, I had one role to play. Tip off the *right* feds and let Hawk handle the rest. I assumed he would be called in to do all the G.I. Joe type stuff. My main objective was to cover Evana and get her to safety after the shoot. My body had other ideas about staying relaxed. My overactive brain had me gauging every possible scenario.

The jungle shoot crew were piled in at the front munching on snacks, chattering away. The radio hummed with the latest chart-popping tunes. I assessed everyone on the bus. Hair stylist, make - up artist, four models, the main photographer, and Maurice. Nothing suspicious at that point. Hawk mentioned this Viper guy coming in for a hit. The whole thing had me on edge and I was sworn to secrecy. I couldn't freak Evana out. My heart had been racing the entire morning. Rumblings in his assassin networks were circulating about his handiwork. Hawk and Viper's paths never crossed, but his reputation preceded him. My eyes were darting all around the bus looking for potential clues. My red jacket, a.k.a super cape, was on. The rest of me was in black... I had the minia-ture spy camera on deck. The one gifted to me by Hawk. James Bond, eat your heart out.

Camera equipment laid stacked precariously in the back of the minivan. Maurice was yakking to the photographer, waving his hands expressively, asking the particulars of the shoot. It was unusual for Maurice to be on site for the shoot. He normally was in the office and didn't come out. As the director, he was responsible for keeping the fashion networks in place and scouting new talent. I wondered if he suspected something. He didn't know the finer details. I fed Maurice breadcrumbs, only the basics of the case. One, for protection, and two, so he wouldn't lose it and potentially blow my cover.

Hawk would be at the park scoping it out. In fact, Norvin State Forest would be right in his element. The great outdoors would take him back to his army days and training camp. For me, I wasn't a fan of chasing a baddie through scrub and woodland. *No, siree. Especially an assassin.* I would rather point and shoot if pressed. Not that I even wanted to do that. I had been to the gun range a time or two to learn how not to shoot myself in the foot. The pure basics. All in all, I wasn't a bad shot. I didn't want to find out how that translated to real life, though. I preferred to use my mental game to solve cases, not my physical. Evana shattered my train of thought.

"Am I staying with you at your place?" Evana whispered anxiously in my ear. We were sitting side by side in the mini-van, she was shaking her knee up and down. I kept looking at it and wished she would stop. The action was making me extra nervous.

"No, my place isn't necessarily safe right now," I murmured softly. My body tensed up as I released the infor-mation. Evana knew nothing of the stakes encased around her. She was in grave danger. Once I knew who wasn't corrupt in the NYPD, I would hand it all over. With copies in my back pocket of course, they knew not to cross me. I would store them separately somewhere.

"What the fuck?" Evana swore, making a distorted face. "He got to you, too! *We are all fucking dead!* I told you he will always find you. The guy is ruthless!" Evana pressed her fingers like claws around my wrist, starting to shake it. I had to peel her fingers back. She had dug so deep, it left tempo-rary red marks around my wrist. I patted Evana's thigh to pacify her. I scanned the bus to see if anyone heard, but everyone continued talking, laughing, or eating. One of the models wasn't laughing as much as I noticed. Sitting silent. Hmm. We were about fifteen minutes from location.

"Calm down." I spat lowly through gritted teeth. "I have backup on location."

I weighed up telling her about the Viper. From her current reactions, I knew she would fully lose it. So, I kept that one up my proverbial sleeve. Even though inside I was thinking, *Run! Run for your fucking life!* We reached the park in good time. Instantaneously the air felt different. Fresh unpolluted oxygen that reminded me that we were out of New York city limits. We were entering the great outdoors. We all poured out of the minivan and stepped into the Norvin State Forest car park.

The photographer, Sven, grabbed all the equipment from the back of the van as all the models gathered themselves and stretched out. Over 5,000 hectares of State Forest encircled us. Making us an easy mark for the Viper, if you asked me. A sanctuary for birds and other creatures, they called it. I contemplated what type of creatures. I wondered if I would want to be eaten by bears or torn to shreds by the Viper. Both choices held no appeal to me.

What a headline. *Vogue Crew including supermodel eaten by bears in Norvin State Forest, what a tragedy.* Not so farfetched in my mind as we passed a Bear Swamp Farm along the way. So clearly bears existed in the park. *Yeesh.*

We were parked at the Otter Hole parking lot, which was the main entrance to the park. Two spots with an orange reserved sign were for us. The air smelled clean and crisp; the skyline blanketed in sky blue. I heard the sound of water gushing. *A brook.* I studied the map before we arrived and saw there were numerous bodies of water in the park. The New Jersey Division of Parks and Forestry knew that we were coming. The car park was small; a couple of hikers appeared to be there already. And one lone black truck. An opening lay right up ahead with sparse grey trees surrounding it. Low level tufts of golden grass were accompanied by a plethora of lichen-covered rocks.

The brook housed several gigantic logs that held their weight against the rushing stream, acting as bridges across the navy water. The park wasn't so green, being it was the height of summer, but sprinkles of it still existed. The light hit the water just right, making it look like stars were floating through it. I honed in on the green parts. *Was that poison ivy?* Apparently, the park was notorious for it. Hopefully the natural elements didn't break us before the Viper did. I wanted to get the shoot done and get the hell outta Dodge.

My pants pocket vibrated. I had my phone on silent. I noticed Maurice's lingering gaze on me. At the time, I didn't pick up on why. I stepped away from the group as the photographer rounded up the four models, relaying the brief of the shoot. Makeshift chairs were set up in the car park ready for the models to be made over. One hairstylist and one makeup artist. Both were busy diving into their kits, ready to prepare jungle looks they needed the models to emulate. I looked closely at my phone.

I'm around you. Just press 7 if you get in trouble. Don't try to text. So far so good. Keep watch. Once the shoot is done. I will follow you and pick you up back at the office. Hawk.

Ok. Let's get through this.

Roger that. I got your back.

My phone continued to vibrate. *What the fuck.* I watched Evana; her makeup was being set in place along with the rest of the girls. Every now and then she would shoot me a pensive look coupled with a furrowed brow. I threw back a smile as best I could. Twenty minutes later, four models were lined up in chairs with full jungle looks. What a crazy sight if you were a passerby. Smatterings of people were either entering the trail path or coming back. They were looking on with curiosity. A creepy peace hung over the place, a weird feeling that held no explanation. Maurice gave me a cutting look. He stroked his chin in a funny way. His movements were disturbing me. When I caught him eyeballing me, he quickly darted his eyes elsewhere. *You're up to something, sucker. And when I find out...*

I checked my phone as I crunched my shoes through the grass to get some space. If a bad guy was coming to kidnap Evana, this would be a great place to start from. You wouldn't even have to leave the park. Walking trails were dispersed across the whole park, but we were at the base and near the closest water source. Sven didn't want the models venturing too far.

"Ewww. I'm not cut out for this model stuff," I grumbled unceremoniously.

A text came from an odd number. I read it twice.

Hurry. Come get me. They're coming for me. I'm scared. I finished the prototype; watch Channel 4. 5 p.m. 8 Clovelly Lane. I have a couple of hours. I stalled them. Shit, shit, shit. Dean Noble, the kid from the burner phone I gave him. Just as I was about to blast off a text to Hawk, he beat me to the punch.

I'm on the road. Limited window to DN. Remember 7. Watch your boss. He's off.

Watch your boss. I was right. *How could he see that?* That peculiar feeling I got around Maurice *was* something. Evana sought out my eyes; she was dressed in a cheetah-inspired jungle print pantsuit. I went to her, zipping up the back of her outfit. I still had assistant duties to perform. All the girls were used to getting dressed out in the open. I covered their modesty with a wimpy towel... One of the models with platinum blonde hair insisted on dressing in the toilet block. I spoke into Evana's ear.

"Stay calm. As soon as this is over, we're outta here." I was trying to lighten the mood; it wasn't working. She threw me a worried smile, her eyes reflecting the immense pain she was in.

She couldn't call in, otherwise it would raise the alarm with Elliot. She was working to keep the same schedule, so he didn't suspect. She was not only beautiful, but a trooper. Evana followed my lead. I felt responsible for her. To make sure I kept her safe from harm. To make sure no people were being destroyed at the hands of Elliot, including myself.

"Ok, ladies. Let's go right over there to the farthest log. Might be a little tricky, but we can pull it off." Sven pointed to a section of the brook with the trees descending over the water in perfect unison. The girls were wrapped up in blankets to keep warm. *Time check.* 3.40 p.m., and we were just getting started. Two of the girls were shivering as the temperature dropped. I wanted to check the energy from Maurice. To see where the side eye stemmed from. He hung back behind everyone gazing around the park. Particularly to the toilet block. I grabbed some water for the girls from the van. It was my excuse to walk behind him and see what his problem was. Maurice saw me walking back to the van.

"Why do you need to go back to the van?" A grimace came over his face.

"I'm getting some water for the girls, so they don't dehydrate." My tone dripped sarcasm. Maurice caught my attitude and stared through me like glass.

"It's quite warm out here. Go ahead." Maurice didn't take his eyes off me as I entered the back of the van to retrieve the box of water. I handed the cups to Maurice as he stood watching. Might as well put him to work. His mannerisms were edgy. *What was going on?*

"Hey Maurice, how's things? Haven't seen you around the office lately. Are you working on new opportunities?" Maurice threw me a pained look as if it was a chore to speak to me and whispered.

"Nice jacket. When will you be off the case? It's disruptive to the girls. I was going to address it with you after this." One minute he seemed excited to have me on board and now the flip. *What changed?* I thought my presence was helpful. I had taken a liking to the role.

"You didn't mention this earlier. Plus, I must talk to my client. I do have some leads that shouldn't take more than a couple of weeks." I delivered my message calmly and steadily. I studied him. He had a deranged look on his face. My skin felt like it was crawling. Shit. Where was this feeling coming from?

"Are you alright, Maurice? You look pale."

He squinted and scowled. "Just focus on getting the girls prepared. At least do that job. I got the cups." He snapped and shooed me ahead to the girls and the brook.

"Ok, ok, Mr. Grumpy Pants." I stuck my tongue out at him and kept moving. I didn't wait to see his reaction. I rubbed the back of my neck and scanned the park. No one but us in this section of the park. No known predators that my eye could see. That was the problem. *That my eye could see. My second pair of eyes, Hawk was gone.* I wanted an update about Dean, but I knew I had to wait. I had to stay dialed in and get Evana through this shoot to safety.

Evana looked every bit the forest tiger in her jungle print. She straddled over the log making claw fists with ease. I peeked at the shots from behind the photographer. The lighting made the scene look otherworldly. Streaks of sun beamed through the trees creating a magical effect. Sven knew his craft well. The next girl up; the platinum blonde, wearing a blue spotted pantsuit. In her hair she sported pale blue extensions. I guess for effect and part of the wild look. She was taller than the rest of the girls. Long-limbed, extremely well-toned, more like an athlete rather than a model. Maybe Sven wanted the athletic look to add diversity. She looked different to the other models. They appeared to be meek pussy cats next to her. The shoulder development of this model was extraordinary. Sven asked her for her best cat pose. She poked her tongue out and positioned herself on the log with perfect balance and her legs spread open. Both of her arms hung straight down in front of the log. She stared straight at me. Her eyes almost looked jet black. She made me uncomfortable for some reason.

I grabbed my throat and moved my eyes away. A queasy feeling came over me. Something was desperately wrong, and I had to figure out what it was. Who was this model? I checked the run sheet. I saw three models listed. Not four. A throbbing began in my chest. My fingers ran again over the run sheet in case I missed it. I knew the other two girls; I had been on location with them. Not this one. I would have remembered her. Her features were strong. She possessed a square jaw and super high cheekbones. A long petite nose and small lips. Still feminine in a lot of ways, but with highly masculine attributes. I watched her foot placement as she slid along the log. Balancing as if she owned the log. *A female Tarzan.* Sven lapped it up.

That's it – become one with the log. You've done this before. You're a pro. I'm glad you got added to the shoot. The new model threw her head back, laughed while baring her teeth. Two of them were like razors jutting down. Almost like a tiger's teeth. Nobody caught it but me. The laugh was throaty, husky almost like a man's, but not quite. Think Eartha Kitt.

Meanwhile, Evana made her way down to me. She had finished her portion of the shoot. Maurice idled at my shoulder, thrusting Evana a drink of water. Maurice kept rubbing his head and observing the girl on the log. How did he know this girl? My arm hairs were in a soldier position. I had a bad feeling. I watched the girl. She resembled a cat. Her movements were stealthy, like those of a ninja. It was mesmerizing to watch – you couldn't look away. I could see Sven's fascination with her.

"Now, ladies, I want the three of you in the shot. That was incredible. What's your name again? I can't remember ever working with you?" Sven gushed. The blonde had him wrapped her finger.

"Svetlana. I would have remembered working with you, too." A deep throaty Russian accent came from the log.

"Mm, mm, Svetlana. Ok. Well, if you keep serving up those looks, we might be working together more often." Sven grinned from behind the camera. Svetlana smiled. Maurice launched into a mini coughing fit at the same time. I was perturbed, and it had a lot to do with this woman. I kept watching Maurice and his shiftiness. Evana stood beside me as she sipped her water. I kept her close. Maurice was on the other side of me.

Sven happily clicked away, oblivious to the tension. *Good. That's brilliant Rose. Really work that neck. Turn to the back for me.* Fifteen minutes later and the girls were all back from the logs.

Sven reviewed the shots, getting ready to pack up. The platinum blonde was behind me which gave me the willies. I heard her flirting with Sven. The other girls were getting changed on the spot. No shame. Maurice spoke in low conversation to the other guy on deck, asking about makeup. General chit chat stuff. More shiftiness. Evana took a sip of her water, her face dreamy with glassy eyes, not so tense. Her face seemed a little slack. Weird, but I took this as a good sign. Maybe the outdoors had calmed her down. Not long to go now. We had about 300 meters to go before we reached the minivan. Svetlana, the creepy blonde, edged up next to me. *How did she do that?* I didn't even see, feel or hear her. She was neck and neck with Evana. Suddenly she grabbed her hand, skipping at high speed, dragging Evana along with her. My eyes were wide open. A split second – gone. That's all it took.

"Let's skip back to the van Evana, such a wonderful shoot." Svetlana let out an evil laugh.

Evana had no words to reply, she just started skipping with her. Except her feet were dragging. She didn't seem coherent. Almost like she had been transported somewhere else. The others were talking casually and slowly making their way to the van. Like this twilight zone scene wasn't in front of their face. I gathered that all kinds of things went on at model shoots, so maybe this was the norm.

"Wait!" I didn't want to blow my cover, but this woman was up to something and Evana didn't look crash hot.

"C'mon then. Catch up." The platinum blonde sang out over her shoulder with her blue extensions fanning in the wind. Evana stumbled like she might fall. I caught up by running. We were steps from the van now and way ahead of the rest of the crew.

"Hey, what the fuck are you doing?" I sounded off in anger. The woman snapped her neck around violently. The octave of her voice deepened, her teeth were bared, her eyes, wild.

"Get in the van now, bitch! Before I take your head off and slit your friend's throat wide open."

Before I had time to defend myself, she shoved me with such force I nearly headbutted the other side of the van. Evana came after me. In a split second, I realized she'd been drugged. Her body was limp, and already in the back slouched across the seats. This wasn't a woman, it was the Viper. *Fuck.* The Viper glanced back at the others. I managed to lift my head briefly to look out the side of the van. I caught sight of Sven the photographer. He saw what was happening; he was hurtling towards us at top speed with arms flailing.

"Hey what the-!" I could hear footsteps running in the direction of us. Yelling and screaming. My head was pounding from the run in with the van door. I felt a slick substance sliding down the top part of my face. Blood. I wanted to cry, but I couldn't. I didn't want this thing to see. The Viper was miles ahead, he slammed the van side door shut and was in the driver's seat in no time.

"So long, bitches. Haha." She laughed and hit the accelerator out of the park. Dust and pebbles kicked up, flying everywhere as the tires screeched.

"Who are you? You won't get away with this!" I shouted from the back. My voice was weak, but I gave it everything. I tried to get up, but the momentum of the vehicle spinning out of the park kept me on top of Evana. She wasn't stirring.

"Ooooo, now I have two to play with. This is going to be good," the woman snarled.

"What did you do to her?" I shouted out.

"She'll be fine. You've got your friend Maurice to thank for that." The Russian accent was gone and replaced with a thick Texan accent of a male.

My mind connected the dots. *That's* why Maurice looked so shifty. He drugged Evana. My mind flashed to the cup of water he gave her. Ten minutes to kick in. *Holy shit.* I pressed my boob where the camera was while I was sideways. I hoped it would pick up the inside of the van and get a read on this thing/man/woman. I wanted badly to pull my phone out of my pocket and press seven, but the Viper's soulless eyes were laser focused on me through the mirror. I couldn't move. I had my gun. I just had to wait for the right moment.

"If you even think of doing anything, I will cut out your pretty little eyes and feed you to the bears. You would be a tasty meal. So, sit back and enjoy the ride."

A moan of despair and disorientation came from Evana's lips. We were either heading North onto Otter Hole Road or South onto Glenwild Avenue. I couldn't tell which, but I knew we were headed for a showdown.

Lucky, I had my super cape on. I was going to need it.

20

HAWK

B irds and wildlife with their promises of song circled Norvin State Forest. Nature always had the answers I sought since I was a little boy. The wind was still and the air crystal clear. I crouched low with binoculars in hand. My semi-automatic was loaded. The dress code consisted of army green and black. Hidden in the shadows of the golden grass, I watched and waited. Quiet out there, peaceful. I could commune with my ancestors. In my mind's eye, I sent my hawk to oversee the land and fly back to me with the truth.

I knew the model's van would be pulling in at approximately 1530 hours. I tracked the van the whole way. I installed a tracking device underneath, when I heard Sara received the assignment brief from Vogue. A few steps ahead were always good. My government contact was applying pressure; they wanted me to get the prototype out of the kid's hands... yesterday.

We've given you enough time. Get that prototype to us immediately! No ifs ands or buts. You have 48 hours to report. That should give you more than enough time.

I linked the burner phone that Sara gave to Dean Noble with mine. As soon as she got news from the kid, I would have it, too. More waiting. I hated that part.

I wanted to make sure Evana and Sara got to safety. The Viper was out there. I ran a check on the Viper through my associates. Guys that worked in the field like me. All of them reported back the same thing. 'This thing' was neither man nor woman and could merge into anything if need be. No, not like a Marvel comic – more like costumes, voices, mimicking, facial reconstruction, that type of thing. So, I was looking for both genders.

The van rolled in right on time. Little did they know I was right underneath their noses. I was on the high left of the park watching through super laser focused binoculars. I could see everything in finite detail. Evana. Beautiful, yet apprehensive, chewing on her nails like she did when she was nervous.

Flashback.

In the kitchen watching her get ready for a Vogue shoot, she bit her nails then. She was fretting about her photographer as he was the best in the business.

"You got this. I believe in you. I know you're going to smash it outta the park."

"You're always so supportive, babe. Thank you."

Those were our happier times. I wished I could reassure her now that everything was going to be alright. But I didn't know that. I knew I would give it everything, though. This Viper thing was an unknown. The other three models exited. Two lithe in build, wispy creatures. The other one, though, strong and well built. I zoomed in closer. Strong jawline. Out of place. Her eyes were circling the park, while the others were focused on getting changed. *Strange. One to watch.* Maurice talked to her with animated hands. Serious glares between the two. Maurice appeared to be high strung and skittish. He was involved somehow with something. My hawk senses told me so. I fired off a text message to Sara to watch him. I was about to examine the strange athletic model when a text rang out from the kid to Sara. I saw it. Time to go. Address was locked in. I had to leave. I made some fancy footwork down the trail undetected, which was fine because all the models were headed to the location of the Otter Hole brook. I slipped out in my black truck.

Less than two hours to get to the kid before Elliot's team did. The saving grace was that Elliot didn't know about me. Likely in his head he had this deal sewn up. It was looking like an easy win for him. Didn't count on the Hawk descending on him. I made quick work of the freeway, speeding in parts, slicing and dicing between the traffic. I called him from a burner phone that couldn't be traced.

"Hey, kid. This is Hawk."

"Huh?" The kid sounded confused.

"Hawk. It's ok – I'm a friend of Sara's," I replied with ease.

"Oh. Ok. I guess." The kid seemed a little calmer.

"So hey, you got a time limit on when they are coming your way?"

"No, the house is bugged, can't talk." Dean's voice trembled. He sounded like he'd been crying.

"Don't worry – they can't track this phone. Stay chill. You like video games, kid?" I tried to keep him placated 'til I got there.

"Yeah, I love them. Been kinda busy lately so I haven't been able to play like I want. Threats of being killed will do that to a kid." He responded with nerdy wit. I laughed. The kid was funny. Especially considering the conditions.

"Ok, so what's this about a leak?" I enquired. I drove fast. I was about half an hour away, weaving through Teaneck, New Jersey. I was trying to get a lead on Elliot's location so I could see how much time I had to get to the kid.

From my satellite read, I had Elliot's location at his house. He was sending his goons out to pick up the kid. Clope and crew, I suspected. Government espionage live and direct right in the backyard of New York. Civilians were going about their mundane lives while evil hid in plain sight. Elliot needed this kid for the deal. Dean was the only one that knew how to run the operation start to finish and set up the satellite. Once they knew how to do that, the kid would be eliminated. *D-E-A-D*, like Sara's client, Michael. The man who knew too much. On the other hand, if they were smart, they would hold the kid and have him create more prototypes. My hawk senses told me it was a one-time deal. What was Elliot up to?

"Sure. We can talk. They call in every ten minutes to see. My mom's at work right now." Little man started sniffling. His sobs were stifled through the phone. He was trying to not cry.

"Hey bud, I got your back. You're not dying on my watch." I spoke to him softly.

"O-kkk. Please hurry, man."

"So, go ahead. Tell me," I coaxed.

"Well, they made me get a read on the Government official from Baltimore. He goes to this club all the time. I had to get video footage together for it and send it across as a test run. They sent it to the news station and are going to leak it tonight. He was exchanging something as well." *World chaos.* Elliot was letting everybody smell his armpits. This was all about Elliot's ego. I shook my head. The media was about to have a field day with this. My superiors wouldn't be happy, but once I got a hold of the kid, I would give them the heads up.

"Ok, you did good, kid. Sit tight, be there in five. I will knock three times. Only open the door when you hear that."

"Hurry up!" Panic was setting in for the kid.

I-95 gods were letting me pass. The run was smooth. Close to 1700 hours, no word from Sara. That model and Maurice. Something eerie. *That wasn't a model.* My hawk senses told me that it was the Viper. Through the binoculars, I saw the calf definition. Masculinity. The hip to waist ratio seemed too narrow. A small puckering in the skin near the top of the forehead was visible. A wig or a lace front. I could pinpoint it through the binoculars. I told Clemens to hit seven on the speed dial if she was in trouble. I tried her phone. *Voicemail.* Problem No. 2. A flash of six ravens circling over an old outhouse was being shown by spirit to me now. My visions were getting clearer. The same premonition since last week. *Sara and Evana were in trouble.* I might not have time to drop the kid off anywhere. *Shit.*

Finally, I turned right into suburbia, nothing of note in this suburb. Quiet, cookie cutter houses, trees lined along the streets. Everybody was tucked away, nobody was out. One man putting his trash out for collection, that was about it. My hawk eyes swept the surface of the space. Nothing. I felt like I had minutes to spare for some reason. I knocked on the door three times like we talked about. A scared weedy nerd answered the door. His eyes darted around me and he looked up at me.

"Whoa. Are you some kind of superhero?" He was in awe, but still shaken. I played along.

"I'm more known as most people's worst nightmare. Not really the hero sort."

"Ok. I feel safe. The prototype is downstairs." The kid raced away, and I heard him tramping down the stairs to get it. The prototype was small. Not huge like you might think. A small black hardware drive that was easily transportable. Who knew something so small could rock a nation with its contents.

"Ok, take anything you want. Grab light things only. We might not be back here for a while."

"Are you serious?" The kid looked torn.

"Yes, kid – I'm serious. You wanna live, right?"

"I guess I do. Alright." He shrugged his shoulders and ran to collect his things.

I wanted to leave a note for the parents to let them know their kid was safe, but I knew we could worry about that later. I slipped on my leather gloves, leaving a feather I found from the park as a signature for the goons. Not a hawk feather, they're not that easy to find. I left a white one instead. The morons would be too dumb to pick up on it. The kid had his laptop underneath his arm and a bulging backpack. We headed to the car. The whole thing took about three minutes to wrap up. I left a bug underneath the couch. I wanted to hear what the goons had to say when the kid they came to kidnap wasn't there. Suckers. I drove out as the perps rode in. They drove straight past my black Jeep.

"Omigod, that's them! The kid slouched voluntarily in the seat.

"Just act normal. They don't know about me. They don't know somebody is looking for you. Wave to your friends." I chuckled.

The boy looked at me in mass confusion. He was about to put up his hand to wave. I grabbed it quickly and put it down.

"Sorry, bad joke." I shouldn't have messed with the kid while he was in distress.

"Ah, ok." My jokes were lost on him. Sara usually got them. Maybe my timing was slightly off.

"I'm taking you to my place and dropping you off 'cos I gotta go catch some baddies." The kid nodded his head in recognition.

"So, here's the deal. I got a fully stocked fridge, go for your life. Keep shit clean. I know you have a laptop, but they will trace you. These bad guys have a lot of money. So, you're going to hand it over and you can use one of mine for the time being."

"But-" The kid went into protest mode.

"You know this already. No negotiation on this one. You

wanna stay alive, right?" I glanced over and raised my eyebrows.

"Yeah, I do. I was going to say I can block their traces." Kid might come in handy. We might be able to do some work together once this was all over. Then again, the kid was set for Harvard; I'm sure they would have better things for him to do. That's if he made it there...

"Hmm. Handy, but let's not risk it this time. The laptop I'm giving you is brand new. It's set up for gamers. So, you oughta like it."

"Whoa! Cool! The Alienware?"

"Yeah, Alienware." For all his nerdy intelligence it was good to see he was still a kid at heart.

I drove quickly to my place and dropped him off.

"Check in with me if anything seems suspect, ok?"

"Bet." He was already getting set to work on the new computer I gave him.

Now time to tackle problem number two...

An assassin that liked to play dress up.

GOOD EVENING, I'm Gunther Roberts, and this is news for now on Tuesday June 14th, 2019. First up, we'll talk about the weather. It's been clear blue skies today and high summer temperatures. Expect more of the same tomorrow. We could hit the upper eighties. Phew, it's hot out there. Stay hydrated, folks. Let's turn now to the case of a New York government official who we won't name, until he's officially identified. This New York official was caught exchanging what looks to be a briefcase and a stash of money. Now it's not clear what is in the briefcase, but the government official opened the case and stacks of white bricks were seen. We'll let you be the judge. These are serious allegations and the video footage is extremely clear. Currently the channel is working to get in contact with the man from the video. This video was leaked to Channel 4 late afternoon from a reputable source. The second video shows the same government official at Sapphires Gentlemen's Club receiving a lap dance from several women. The alleged official is running for New York City Mayor in the next local election. More to come on this in the next few hours as we try to locate the government official in question for an explanation.

21

SARA

T he road felt different than the one we drove in on. That's the first thing I noticed. The sounds around the vehicle were different. I sat up in the seat now that the car had stopped its swerving. The others knew the van had been taken over by a maniac. This maniac was bold enough to take photos and be present in a fashion shoot. I had nothing to lose, so I started asking questions.

"Are you the Viper?" I quizzed. Evana was still out cold beside me murmuring in her drug induced slumber.

"How do you know that?" I was met with those vacant eyes in the mirror. The Russian voice came back. Multiple personalities. *Oh boy*. It was going to be a long ride. She stopped the vehicle on the side of the road. I took in the scene as fast as I could: yep, Glenview.

"I'm whatever you want me to be. Put your seatbelt on, bitch." Concern for my safety. Well this was a first.

"Your face is all over the shoot. You know there's probably a police squad after you right now." I pointed out the obvious. I looked at Viper square on in the front mirror. A soulless ghoul peered back at me.

"I never lose. Plus, we are switching cars, you dummy." The Russian accent held steady in place.

"Give me your phone." The Viper's claws beckoned for the phone. Ugly veined hands with talons. Gross.

"What phone I don-" I was trying to stall her. If she had my phone, I had no way of reaching Hawk.

"GIVE ME THE FUCKING PHONE!" The Viper's eyes blazed with anger, bringing nauseating fear that rendered me speechless. I handed over the phone to her – or it, should I say. Hard to say who or what this thing identified as. Either way it was terrifying. The Texan accent came back. Sounded like a man. Hawk had to find us. I had supreme faith in him. The Viper snatched my phone and slid it in her bra. No chance of digging my hands in there. It wasn't that serious. The Viper turned off on East Shore Road. I remembered from the map that we were still close to the park. I could see the main road from the turn off and a Ranger vehicle went past. My throat keep closing shut and opening as I watched the vehicles stream by. Then another. Ok. Locals were looking for us. That was a positive sign.

Please. Help. Please. Don't let us die out here with this thing...

"Get her out of the back and get in the car." A black Chrysler 300 was parked, waiting for us. I gave Evana a light tap on the face. *Wake up. C'mon Evana.* I looked at the Viper through the van window and worked to lift the dead weight of Evana from the van. Her feet clip-clopped over the van ledge. She weighed a ton. Faint whimpers escaped from her lips. It's like she was stuck in a place of semi consciousness. The next moment was one I would never forget.

The Viper placed his fingers at the top of his hairline and slowly pulled off a face mask. It came off in globs. I was abhorred with what I was seeing. My eyes struggled to process it all. Sounds of forest trees rustled with the wind singing through them. A raven's call sounded off in the distance Underneath the mask was a man. An effeminate man, but a man all the same. He unclicked dentures from his mouth, saliva dripped from the corners revealing a tight greasy smile. Yellow teeth remained. Hairpin thin eyebrows. A sharp pointy nose. His features resembled that of a rat. I liked him better as Svetlana.

"Glad those suckers are out." The Texan accent returned with force.

"They were a bitch to get in." A heavy Texan drawl. This guy was nuts. Certifiable.

"What the hell you looking at? Get her in the car, now." The Viper had a pistol tucked underneath the jungle suit. *That's why he changed in the bathroom.* Pieces of the rubber mask were still stuck to the thing's face. Stubble. Dark lifeless eyes. A scar at the top of the forehead. Dark brown hair. I was taking in as much as I could. Before I could do anything else and plan to draw my gun, a bottle swept under my nose. My world faded to black.

I didn't know how long it took me to come to. My head was groggy when I woke up. My feet were immovable. They were bound in a fish knot with heavy duty rope. I was bound and gagged in a chair. My hands were tied in front of me, not behind the chair. The blindfold had been lifted from my eyes. The roof was open. Looked like half of it had been blown off in a tornado. My red jacket was still intact. I wasn't feeling my superpowers right now. My body ached, and an acute pain stabbed through my head. Hawk couldn't be far away. The sky was painted slate grey. A couple of hours at most before it would be completely jet black. I saw floorboards as I looked down. A couple of rats scurried across the floor to their home in the wall. Next to me, Evana was held in the same position. Side by side. A single lightbulb that was extremely bright glowed in our faces as we sat directly under it.

The repulsive weasel paced the floor. The Viper. A shadow

of black. Red-rimmed and glassy eyes. A pistol. No torture tools from first glance. Evana shook her chair, rocking back and forth to move. No point. A total waste of energy. I swiveled my head to her, widening my eyes for her to sit still. Tears formed in her eyes. The distress was written all over her. I knew what she didn't, though. I raised my head to the sky. Six ravens were circling. What made it spooky was the sequence they moved in. All flew in a perfect circle. My eyes were straining to make them out as the sky bloomed in darkness.

"Ah, she awakens." The Viper was swinging his pistol. Twirling it around his finger. Once I saw the sky, a peaceful energy filtered to me. I knew Hawk would find us now. Hawk always told me when the ravens circled it was his spirit guide protection. *He was close.* We were somewhere significant. Every cell in my human vessel knew it. The Viper didn't know. Neither did Evana.

"Before I kill all y'all, how about a little playtime. Let's call your li'l boyfriend, shall we? Miss Thang in the Red Jacket." A heavy Texan drawl. Wait. The man had breasts. Fake, but still they were prominent. No wonder he wasn't easy to catch. What gender did the Viper operate under? Obviously took his job seriously. He pulled my phone out of his bra.

"Looky, looky through the Little Black Booky. Hmm. Last caller. Speed Dial seven. That's a good one. Done that one myself. You tried to trick me." The weasel pierced his malevolent gaze through me. He smiled at Evana, licking his lips, the explosive rage I held inside wanted to pummel this guy into the ground.

"You sho' is cute. Could just eat you up." More licking his crusty lips... This thing was a reptile. I felt my stomach wanting to heave.

"Let's put him on speaker, shall we? We all want to hear. I don't want y'all to miss a thing. Might even let him listen to the gunshot." The ravens were squawking.

"Damn birds, been doing that for the last fucking hour. I wish they would shut the hell up." The birds were really getting under his skin. Good. Distraction. I surveyed the room. He found my gun. It was on the table next to his. He saw me look.

"Oh, that's so sweet you had a Smith and Wesson. See, brilliant for me. You're going to kill Evana with your gun, and then you're going to kill yourself. It's going to be a murder-suicide."

The Viper clapped his hands together, his red-rimmed eyes gleaming. "I'm feeling a little nice, so I will untie your hands. Right before I take you out. I'm a really good guy." I didn't want this thing touching me, but at least our hands would be free. My head felt like it was on fire, but my sense of justice and kicking this thing's ass made the pain bearable. I knew if we made one wrong move, though, he would shoot us both dead. He moved to me first and untied my hands. His touch sent ripples of disgust up my spine. I rubbed my wrists where the rope had dug in.

"Hurt?" The Viper smiled, baring his ugly wolf teeth. I didn't answer.

He moved to Evana next, she moaned, recoiling from him as he approached. He flicked his tongue out at her. She massaged her wrists; he had tied hers tighter than mine. The weasel, I noticed, had on white gloves. He clapped and flipped his foot out in a weird dance. The guy was a mental case. No prints. A protective sheet covered the ground we were on and the place smelled of bleach. He was covering tracks and setting things up. I snarled under the gag.

"Sometimes my job is so much fun. Ok. Enough with that. Let's make the call."

The shrill tone of the phone ringing rang out. Two rings, Hawk answered. Silence. Smart move.

"Hawkkkkkkyyyy, come out and play. I know it's you." The ravens were still squawking. I closed my eyes in disgust.

"What do you want arsehole?" The weasel's thin brows lifted.

"Oh, so you know who I am? Kudos to you. Your sexy friends are here. We are having ourselves a little reunion. I've heard about you, too. Say you're the best in the biz. Pity you been caught slipping. Shame I gotta put a bullet hole in both your girls' heads. Might have some fun with the model first. The other one is no good." Evana shrieked and became hysterical. The Viper laughed with glee in response.

A shadow at the back of the building went by. My heart lurched. A human figure. Guess who?

22

HAWK

♟

I was on the move. Two ways outta Norvin State Forest. Well three, really. Into the State Park itself. Doubtful. Too risky for the Viper. Rangers were scattered all around the park. That wouldn't be his move. The radio was on and I clocked onto the news. Just as the boy warned, the leak spilled out. Alleged government official involved in a drug trade and a regular at Sapphires Gentleman's club. Something must have gone wrong for Elliot to oust this guy. Stole some money most likely. Who knows? The kid was good. No doubt a phone call was coming from my superiors about the leak. I chuckled to myself as I watched Elliot's goons pass me when I picked up the kid. *Stupid*. I played back the surveillance tape, listening with one earphone in my ear. I had the tech capabilities to connect my satellites everywhere I went. Including my car.

"Oh shit. Where's the kid? Holy shit. Elliot is going to fucking kill us!" Bozos for real. *Shoulda got their earlier, boys…* I took out the earphones after that – I needed to concentrate. I'd listen to the rest later. I watched the road, deciding the best

course of action was to head back in the direction of the park. As an assassin with Native American roots, my methods were unorthodox, but they worked. I began a chant my Grandfather taught me as I drove.

"Calling in all the Great Spirits of the North, bring me strength. Great spirit of the East, bring me light. Great Spirit of the West, bring me illumination. Great spirit of the South, reveal the earth's plain and the direction I must go. Guide me, Mother Moon and let the truth be unveiled from behind your curtain. Ancestors, send my guides to access the location of Evana and Sara. Offer them peace and protection in their time of need. Thank you."

Moments later, a powerful blue flash pulsed before my eyes. One of the greatest I've seen. I had to pull over to the side of the road. A message was given from the Great Spirit. *Delaware Indians. Delaware, look for the land of the Delawares. The devil lives there. The devil lives there.* The Great Spirit was speaking. I pulled back onto the road. I was about thirty minutes out, give or take, with traffic. I wanted to get to them in time. I didn't know what state they were both in. Sara was a tough cookie, though. If I knew her, she was already working on a master plan. Another flash. A vision. I nearly lost control of the car. I pulled over again.

Siri give me all the regions of Delaware Indians in New Jersey.
Sure. Hopatcong...

The images flashed like a kaleidoscope. A large abandoned warehouse with ravens circling in a formation of six. Both of them were tied to chairs. A dark sinister energy. An entity filled with hate. The model was a man. She was a he. I saw it now. That's how he got away with it all. If the suspect was a female, he portrayed as a man and vice versa. His eyes were black. Pure evil personified. The vision was crystal clear. Six boulders. I knew this region. A face appeared, a Delaware Indian tribesman. Hopatcong. Sacred site. They were upset their region was being disturbed by a madman. Lenai Lenape camps. Visions. I waited. My head was hurting. I stayed with it. Their lives depended on it. Deep breaths. More visions entered. Six boulders again. I opened my eyes with a flurry. *Devil's Footprint.* He had them near Devils Footprint. The Delaware Indians would send a sign when I was close to the location.

Dusk covered the sky and soon it would be dark. I punched the accelerator as fast as I could without alerting the police. I was over the speed limit. I didn't care. A risk worth taking.

I slowed down as I got to Brooklyn Mountain Road. A weird sensation enveloped me. I was close; the sensation led me to the junction of Columbia Trail and Brooklyn Mountain Road. A hawk started to fly beside my car. My sign. It flew across my windscreen to the left. I veered the car left. I dimmed the lights. I got out. I was strapped, ready to rock and roll.

Thank you, ancestors.

I had goggles on my head and a breathing mask around my neck. I had a treat for the Viper. I ran in low. Lights and a barn more so than a warehouse.

Why were the lights on?

This guy was not the sharpest tool in the shed, if you asked me. Asking for trouble. I looked up; six ravens circled the top of the barn. No roof. Black Chrysler. I let the tires down. Stabbed them with my knife. The sound of them deflating was music to my ears. My breathing was heavy. I was close enough to hear voices. The Viper spoke. Texan accent. Now he was Texan? So, he knew how to play characters. The barn was made of timber, no windows on the sides. I ran my fingers along the edge of it. One large barn door. I snuck around the back; it had a large window. They were there, both tied up, looking helpless. Knocked about. My phone vibrated. Shit. The fucker was calling. Perfect timing. I was hoping it didn't echo.

"What can I do for you, arsehole?" I asked smoothly after a few moments of silence. I wanted him to answer first.

"Now that's no way to speak to a friend." A heavy Texan accent responded. One gun on the bench behind him. The other dangling in his hand. The element of surprise would be the way to go here. Time to cut this bullshit conversation short. I kicked the barn door in, dust flew up. The ravens cawed as I threw down a tear gas bomb. Dropped the mask on my face. Twenty paces to the Viper. Thirty to the victims. He saw the smoke first and dropped the phone. He turned, ducked low and fired. Too late: the tear gas was leaking and had the room covered. The bullet whizzed past my ear. He wasn't a bad shot. Not good enough, though.

"You bastard!" the Viper hissed. He was covering his eyes desperately to see through the heavy vapor cloud forming. I kept coming. I was in the clear. I had goggles on and a mask. I was born for these moments. I lived for the glory of destroying vile beings like this.

Arghhh. The shot clock was running I was about fifteen seconds away. Closing in; fifteen paces to the victims. Less to the Viper, more like 10 seconds. I slid a knife and a set of keys like a bowling ball directly to Clemens's chair. She blocked it with her foot. For some reason, he left their hands untied. A part of her hair was matted to her face. That shit pissed me off. I figured their hands being untied was because he planned on killing them quickly. Arrogant fuck. Clemens tipped her chair and picked up the knife. She made quick work of the ties around their feet. *Stupid move. I* thought this guy was supposed to be clinical. *To be precise and clean.* So far, he wasn't living up to his reputation. I saw that he wasn't much of an improviser. If something went wrong in the plan, he couldn't work with that. His plan had come unstuck. The clean getaway wasn't his. Both Evana and Sara were coughing, but making do. Viper was too busy looking at me like a deranged madman. He didn't know what to tackle first; he didn't have time to deal with them.

He fired another round and moved in scurrying on his hands and feet. I knew he couldn't see. He was working on instinct and sound. I looked straight at him and quick drew my tomahawk from my belt girdle. I knew the exact placement where my fingers needed to be to execute the throw. I could throw blindfolded. It hit the target, knocking the gun out of his hand. My tomahawk formed an arc swerving past him to land on the wall. He angled left so he wouldn't get hit. The tear gas left him reeling and gasping for breath. He regained himself well and flew back across the floor like a monkey. The retreat. He was heading for the barn exit.

"Having trouble, Viper?" I sounded like Darth Vader with the mask on. I kept walking towards him at a steady pace.

"Wha--What are you doing, you fool?" His elbow jutted out covering his eyes. He wasn't coping.

"I don't like snakes. I'm cleaning up the yard." He was outside the barn now. No fight back. Interesting. He had no weapons though, so it made sense.

He was retreating to the open which is where I wanted him. That was a two-fold plan. One, to give the girls enough time to reach their cars. Two, to get the Viper into my element. My playground. The outdoors. Finish him off. As soon as he got outside, he escaped. Running. Into the night. I heard him rambling through the thickets of the forest nearby. I winced. That meant I would have to face him again. Next time he wouldn't be unprepared. He knew about me. Couldn't worry about it now.

I had bigger fish to fry. I wasn't about to chase him down. We would face off in the future. That I was certain of. Sara swung the vehicle into view. They made it to the car. I knew she would.

"Let's go!" Sara called out. I raised two fingers.

"Wait!" I ran inside pulling my tomahawk out of the side

of the wall. My grandfather gave it to me. I couldn't leave it. The ravens sat inside the barn now. Watching. Six in a row. Unity. I swear one of them winked. The job was done. I bowed to them and left.

The Viper was dealt with for now, but that wouldn't be the end.

23

SARA

♟

I t was dark inside the vehicle until the dashboard lit up. I was in the driver's seat. I cranked the engine, ready to accelerate out of this hellhole. I felt the roaring anger ripping through my system.

"Elliot's going down. This is the guy he sent? He's going to have to do better than that."

I was pissed. *Beyond* pissed. If I gripped the steering wheel any harder, I would have pulled it off. Hawk came through like he always does. He rubbed my shoulder for encouragement. Evana sat quietly, shell-shocked. She was busy staring hard at Hawk. I thought she might burn a hole through him.

"You ok back there?" I enquired peeping through the mirror. She was a whole mess and then some. She bent to rub her ankles as if she was attempting to rub away the rope burn from her feet. Meanwhile, smeared blood had dried on the right side of my face. I wasn't much better myself.

"I... can't believe this." She threw her hands up in disbelief.

"Hawk? Fucking Hawk? It's you!" Hawk looked at me with a side glance. More connecting the dots. My face drained of color. Hawk asked me all those questions because Evana was the ex he fell in love with. *Oh my God. This guy was good at keeping secrets.*

"Evana, I never meant to hurt you. I just couldn't risk it. Thank me later." Hawk spoke with a softness I only heard occasionally. These guys needed to talk. I felt like I was in the middle of a tragic love story. Why didn't he tell me this? *I mean, what the fuck?*

"I can't deal with this right now." Evana broke down crying, holding her face in her hands.

"You could have told me. Trusted me." She shook her hands.

"You and me both," I shot at Hawk.

"Welp. What was I going to say? Hey, I'm an assassin? You would have laughed me the fuck outta here. Then put you in harm's way on assignments? That's selfish of me," Hawk countered. I gave him a hard backhander with my free hand.

"Ok, I deserved that." Evana couldn't shift her eyes off Hawk. She kept blinking rapidly as if to blink him away. I focused on what had to be done next. We weren't home free yet.

"Ok, Evana we gotta get you on the plane. Hawk you got it set up?" I raised my brows at him in anticipation.

"Yeah, my guy knows. We gotta make a run for it, though. He can't hold the flight. He has a limited window for clearance on the runway. You gotta punch it, girl." Hawk hit the dash with the palm of his hand.

"Ok, let's do this." I pushed the accelerator a little closer to the ground. I didn't know how much Elliot knew. It would take time to get feedback, provided information hadn't been passed to the media. Elliot was always lurking on Evana's shoot. If Maurice opened his mouth, he may already know. Evana watched our interaction like we were aliens.

"Maurice was in on it. He drugged her," I relayed to Hawk. He closed his eyes briefly and balled his fists.

"Are you feeling okay, Evana? Groggy?" Hawk was enquiring after Evana with concern. He still loved her. I could sense it.

"A little foggy in the head. I have a massive crazy headache." She groaned.

"Here, take this." Hawk dug into his pocket and passed her a white pill. I looked at him strangely.

"You just happen to have Advil in your pocket?" I raised one eyebrow. I kept my eyes steady on the road. I was punching 20 above the speed limit. I slowed down, just in case. I didn't want the cops stopping us on the way. That would be a shitstorm and a half.

"I told you to watch him." I felt Hawk's eyes on me.

"I know. I know. I was a step too late." My eyes started to sting from all the concentration. I ducked and weaved between traffic, seeking for the gaps. We were on our way to a secret airfield to get Evana across the seas.

"He drugged me? Why would Maurice..." Evana was discombobulated. She was in deep shock.

"The Viper probably forced him. Had to comply, who knows? We'll get to him later." Hawk eyed her in the mirror.

"Everything's going to be ok. You're going away for a while," I countered.

"Oh my God, my life! What will I do?" She was freaking out. "Can't I just stay here? I can just get a lawyer. I have money!"

"Evana, did you see what Elliot sent for you? Did you see what happened? You're not safe, we just want to get some of the heat off you. Then we can organize for you to come back to the country." Hawk was clear cut: this is what the next part of the plan was.

"You're in good hands. I'm not going to let anything happen to you, Evana. I swear on my Grandfather. Do you trust me?" Evana started weeping into her hands again. I bet she wished she'd never met Elliot.

"Yes. This is... it's too much." I blew out a heavy sigh and searched Hawk's face for solutions.

"Do you have access to your accounts?" Hawk's voice was steady, yet firm. All business. I was coming close to the airfield location.

"Yes, I have my own account. He doesn't have the details. I signed a prenup. He doesn't think I'm that smart," Evana responded in a quivery voice.

"Good." Hawk replied, giving her a warm smile.

"Hawk?"

"Yes, Evana?"

"Thank you." Her watery eyes lifted from her mascara-stained lashes and smiled.

"My pleasure. I'm sorry I didn't tell you." He pleaded with his eyes. This was new. Hawk in a vulnerable state. She had turned the big guy to mush. I kind-a liked it.

"It's ok. I get it." They both let out a little laugh together. Clearly, they still had mad amounts of chemistry. I was happy they patched it up for the sake of the situation.

The airfield in Byram township snuck into view. A pilot in plain clothes was standing in front of a small Cessna, white with blue stripes, and she was ready to fly. Two bulky security guards were next to him. This was it. Evana's getaway.

Evana boarded the plane safely. Hawk kissed her goodbye and gave her a long hug. Well, well. Seems we all had our dirty little secrets. I stared at him for a long moment as he re-entered the vehicle.

"Don't look at me like that. I'll tell you later." Hawk let out a long breath. "I'm just glad she's on the plane."

"You most definitely will tell me all about it. You owe me breakfast, lunch *and* dinner for withholding secrets."

"I got you." He smiled.

"Ok, we've got work to do. The drop is tomorrow. They

have to re-adjust. They don't have the kid. It's going to throw them off. He has a missing supermodel as well. Let's see how he handles it." Hawk was crunching on nuts from his pocket and passed some to me. He poured a few in my hand as I drove.

"I agree. It's a major change in his plans. He's been blind-sided. He can't possibly run the deal now. Evana's free. The kidnapping could be traced back to him."

"Exactly. But he's smart, he hasn't gotten this far without some form of resilience and contingency planning. The Columbians won't let him off that easy. They want what they came for. Suarez ain't a man to renege on." I nodded my head in agreement.

"You're not safe, though. You gotta come to mine for a minute."

"Agreed."

"Hang tight a minute." Hawk raised his hand. His phone was ringing.

"Yep. Secured. Check in three hours. Done."

"Your report?" I queried.

"Yeh." Hawk's face was grim. Not that he was grim. Just his face, he got like this when it was do or die.

We were ten minutes from Hawk's place in Mendham. We were preparing ourselves for war. Time was of the essence. Hawk's place was a little further out than mine. He was about fifty-six minutes from New York City. Technically. Add another thirty minutes to an hour to the needle if traffic was backed up. Hawk told me about the new head of the Narcotics Division and that he was clean. A lot of the cops in the department would be clenching their butt cheeks together because this guy had a reputation for weeding out corruption.

How did Hawk know the guy was clean? He was one of Hawk's counterparts back in the army days. He could safely vouch for him. Small world after all, it seemed.

Hawk turned off the engine and we entered his place.

According to the wire, the deal was going down tomorrow at six. Location was one of three places: the old Donut Factory that Elliot mentioned on the phone, his house, or the warehouse docks he took over. Two of the locations were obvious picks. One was in public and would need a form of security. The other was Elliot's turf. His house. The old donut factory felt like a ploy to throw me off the scent.

Just inside the door posted up at Hawk's kitchen table was Dean Noble. He almost jumped to the ceiling when the door opened.

"Shit! You scared me."

"It's alright. It's just us." Dean looked at us both with the saddest face ever.

"Can I go home now? My Moms will be looking for me. She's a worrier."

"You can soon, buddy. We need to protect you and her. Sit tight and everything will be ok." Hawk went to the fridge and threw water my way.

"You want to freshen up first, then we can get down to it? You need some ice for the lump on your head." I had forgotten about it, so much had happened. I touched my forehead. A nice shiner had developed from the Viper slamming me into the van door. Before I had time to answer, Hawk threw me an ice pack.

"YeAh, I could use a shower." That was an understatement. I smelled like dirt, sweat, and fear. I took the hottest shower I could muster and washed the ick and blood away. My wrists were the telltale sign of the kidnapping. Rubbed red and raw from rough handling. I was eager to go home, but who knew if the Elliot clan ransacked my place or not. Hawk had a bowl of soup in front of him and the kid. One was waiting for me, too. We sat eating in silence for some time. I wasn't exactly comfortable discussing drug operations in front of him, even though the kid was working on a tool of supreme espionage for a crime syndicate. So, Dean knew plenty already.

"Ok kid, we gotta love you and leave for a minute. Be good."

"Ah, ok. Are you leaving again?" He seemed shit scared to be alone. I didn't blame the kid.

"No, we're going downstairs. We won't be far. Right in the house," Hawk replied.

"Phew. Ok." The kid sighed with relief and went back to the game he was playing.

I was puzzled. Were we headed somewhere else, or just another room?

"Follow me." Hawk gestured. He led me downstairs to his basement door. He pressed a place on the side of the wall and a screen popped up.

"What the hell, Hawk?" He put his eyeball up to the screen and a laser beam scanned it. The screen began to talk to him, and he punched in a code. A whoosh sound was made, and the door slid open. I needed time to pick my mouth up off the floor. *This was what he was hiding*! All this time. A secret operations room. Computers were everywhere, printouts were running, code flashed across multiple screens and one huge satellite screen. This was some serious spy shit. I was blown away.

"About time you saw it, I figured." Hawk studied my face.

"Holy shit. This is your own central intelligence unit right here." I gushed. I started touching all the panels and absorbing everything.

"Goes without saying that this place is confidential."

"No shit. This is insane. How long did this place take to build?" I was in awe of Hawk at this point.

"Years." That was his simple ass reply. I needed the breakdown.

"'Kay, so while you're picking your mouth up, here's what

I know. There's a secret room in Robert's mansion. I retrieved the plans from the New Jersey City Council. Pulled the records. See, right here." Hawk pointed to the screen with his finger. Hawk blew up a portion of the screen on one of the smaller computers and it switched to the large screen.

"That's where the Elliot's hold their meetings." I watched carefully as Hawk demonstrated where the hidden rooms were.

"Did I say holy shit before? Let me say it again." Hawk grinned at me. "Badass huh?"

"I'll say."

"That's my pick on the location. There's a new Special Agent in Charge of the U.S. Drug Enforcement team in NYC. I tipped him already by sending the wire taps across. Including the one with Taylor being mentioned."

"Okay, one step forward. It's going to be tough to indict this man." Hawk frowned.

"You're telling me."

"Elliot would have wanted the Columbians on his turf, so he could control the situation. Since he doesn't have the prototype, this might send him off site. Into the open, so if there is bloodshed the carnage isn't linked specifically to him. No trace. This won't be a peaceful affair."

"Or he could just flee? He's done it before. I know evidence wasn't linked to him, but I suspect he had something to do with the college drug ring killings."

"You know about that?"

I gave Hawk an eye roll. "I'm not a shit detective."

Hawk placed his palms up in surrender. He looked impressed. "You're right. Same feeling I had." Hawk mused.

"He could just take off."

"You can't run from the Columbians. He's going to have to come up with something."

"Who's this new agent?" I queried.

"Special Agent Marconis."

"So Marconis knows?"

"Yeh, I'm going to be on location. He's sending a team to the Elliot's on watch and another task force to the docks. I think he'll do it at the docks. He doesn't have a prototype. Covering all bases."

"Wow. And when did you do this?" I was seeing a whole new aspect of Hawk, and he was seeing a new one in me. Revelations all round.

"This is my job. I'm contracted to Homeland Security Investigations for this gig. I've done work for them before. That's one of the reasons why Marconis was willing to listen to me. British Intelligence for the prototype, which I'm due to hand deliver. Two separate gigs, but intricately linked. If you say anything, then of course I have to kill you." Hawk laughed. Assassin humor. I shook my head.

"Are you going to be on ground for this one?"

"Yeh, I am. I'm military trained, so I will be at the docks. I can help in some way. I may be a part of the sniper team. Who knows? See what they've got for me tomorrow."

"How many cops are dirty? If your guy is clean, aren't they going to wanna swarm and get him out?"

"Yes, but Marconis is smart. He has a new team. I sent the files across to him with the dirty cops along with the intel."

"How could you-,"

Hawk smiled. "I have a number of undisclosed sources. Underground."

I had to sit down; my head was spinning. I had the ice pack held above my eye, slowly the lump was reducing in size.

"You're going to be on shortly. We got check in."

"We?" I sang out meekly.

"Yes, Marconis wants to speak to you, too," Hawk was busy pressing buttons on his desk.

"This case!" The sense of being overwhelmed had started to engulf me and I didn't know what to do. The gigantic screen that covered most of Hawk's spy cabin flickered and switched to a boardroom with two men.

"Hi, Hawk. How are you doing, buddy?"

"Hey, Marconis. Looking good. Congrats on your new position. Dermas, nice to see you again." Two middle aged men were sitting at a boardroom table looking back at us. One more relaxed than the other.

"Hawk. Thanks for clocking in."

"Pleasure."

"Hi Sara, we've heard a lot about you." Marconis was talking to me! This whole scene was surreal.

"Uh, hi." I gave them both a tentative wave.

"I need to tell you both. This conversation never happened right from the get-go. No record of it will ever be found. Capiche?"

"Without a doubt." Hawk responded.

"Sara, I want to commend you on your great detective work. If you ever want a job, please let me know. We always need more great detectives on the squad. I know you've had a rough day. But we need more women like you on the right side of the law."

"Thanks, sir. I just like to catch the bad guys." I felt the heat rush to my cheeks. All of them let out a wry chuckle.

"We do, too. Speaking of that, we are ready to roll. Hawk, we need you to come in and report so we can brief you. This won't be an easy bust. Elliot is crafty. We have enough thanks to both of you to implicate Elliot in several crimes. Including his street crew."

"Ok, I'll be ready to go."

"Sara, at this stage you've done your job. You're free to go. We will be talking to you at a later stage about the case." I wanted to breathe a sigh of relief, but somehow, I knew the battle wasn't over.

"What about my house? What if Robert had his goons sent to kill me?"

Dermas piped up. "Hi, Sara, I'm the head of Homeland Security. Your place is safe. We conducted a sweep of it three times. No bugs, no nothing. Clean and clear. No break ins. We are watching your neighborhood just in case. I have a direct line for you to reach if you sense anything is off. The moment you do call me, we won't take it lightly. Elliot is a dangerous man." Dermas was reassuring me that I was okay to head home. I didn't know what to feel at this stage.

"Ok." I blew out a sigh at the news.

"Alright, thank you both. Hawk we'll see you at 6:00 a.m. sharp at base."

"Yessir." The screen fuzzed and glitched out. I keeled over in amazement.

"You are a full-blown double agent. Forget the assassin part!"

"Something like that." Hawk laughed and stretched his long muscular legs.

"One doesn't overlap the other, though. I'm not double-crossing. No espionage is involved. That's Elliot. He's the one implicating government officials; he's nuts. Elliot's let that power go to his head. He's playing with the big boys now."

One thing was lingering over both our heads that we weren't talking about.

"He's still out their Hawk. Or is it a she?"

"Whatever fits for the crime, I'm guessing. You let me handle that one. You feel ok to go home?" Hawk gave me an apprehensive look.

"Yeh, I'll be fine." The adrenalin spike from all the madness had drained my body. I simply wanted a pizza and beer. I had a forty-minute drive to get home yet. I hoped the drive home would have cleared my head. *It didn't.* What was Elliot going to do? How come he didn't come to my house to ransack it? How come he didn't come looking for Evana? I had so many rapid-fire thoughts running through my head. Truth be told, I was shaky. I really didn't want to go inside alone.

I pulled up in my driveway. The streetlights were on. I sat in the car looking at my dark house. I turned my head from left to right to check. I retrieved my keys from my bag in preparation. Eventually, I worked up the nerve to get out of the car. My porch light automatically came on as I got closer to the door. I flipped my head from side to side so many times I reactivated my headache. I quickly put my keys in the door and stopped for a split second. My hands were trembling, but I got there with the keys. I walked in quickly, turning on all the lights with my gun drawn. I was going crazy. Lucky, I got my gun *and* my phone back. Thank fuck, the Viper didn't take those. He would have retrieved my information. To be honest, if he wanted to get it, I'm sure he could.

The issue was the Viper's agreement with Elliot. I let my mind build up in fear of the possibilities. If he was paid upfront then maybe he wouldn't be back for me or Hawk. If he was only paid half and then the other half was dependent on death… He would be back. If he was just a plain psychotic individual who liked to kill, he would be back. The options were too vast for me. Hawk couldn't always be there. Just like he had to leave at the shoot, he might have to do that again. I had to beef up my skills. Maybe I could learn martial arts or something.

I opened my fridge door and the light went on. Two lonely beers. Both were calling my name. Not before I nearly jumped through the roof when the phone rang. I looked at it for several seconds. Elliot? Hawk? Cops? Who the hell was it? I stared at the blue screen: it was Hawk.

"Hey," Hawk said softly. "You okay? I know you're not so that's why I'm ringing you."

"Since you answered for me, what's left to say?" I

unscrewed the lid of my beer and found the fridge magnet to call UberEATS for a pizza.

"Hey, it's going to be alright. Trust me. Like I said to Evana, I'm not going to let anything happen to you." I smiled; Hawk was sweet when he wasn't hiding things.

"You're in a bind yourself, aren't you? What are you going to do about Evana?" Pregnant silence hung in the air.

"Who knows. I don't know what to do. She's landed though. I got a text from my buddy. She's fragile, but safe. I gotta work that one out." I took a gulp of my beer. I felt the mellowing coming.

"You guys belong together," I quipped.

"I don't know. Too much has happened. I don't think we can recover." Hawk was in complete denial about the situation. The love between them was written all over them.

"You love her?" I was digging a little bit now.

"Yeah." Hawk replied like love was a death sentence. In some ways it was. It could get you killed.

"*What!* Hawk, the rogue assassin is in love with someone? Here's one for the record books."

"Don't you start." Hawk chuckled a little. "By the way, I have satellite surveillance on your house."

"Outside or inside?" I asked.

"Outside. I don't want to watch you pee." I nearly spit out my beer.

"Thanks, I'm grateful for that. Hey."

"Yeah?"

"Thanks for saving my life again."

"Never a dull moment. And no problem. Call me if you see anything tampered with."

"Will do. 'Night, Hawk."

"'Night, Ms. Clemens. Stay safe. I changed our code by the way. It's 88 now."

"Ok, perfect."

I ordered a pepperoni pizza, triple locked the doors, checked every room in the house and let my eyelids go droopy. I fell into a deep slumber on the couch. If I had ventured to my bedroom, I would have noticed the piece of stark white paper sticking out from underneath the bed.

24

SARA

♟

I wiped the drool from my face and woke up thrown. *Where was I again?* Oh, that's right. I was on my couch because I didn't make it to the bed. I stretched out my limbs and uncrumpled myself. Today was a huge day. In the back of my mind I wanted to be a fly on the wall for the bust. On the other hand, I was glad to be nowhere near the scene. I was thinking about Elliot. I was employed to solve a murder originally. My client was reasonably satisfied - not that you could be happy your son was dead. I knew who did it. So did my client. He wanted justice, but he knew it wasn't neces-sarily possible. Robert's pull in the city and purse strings were so entrenched it would be difficult to pin him down. Now it was up to the taskforce to bring this man down. The floating body parts were part of the evidence. How deep the corruption ran and how many people were willing to cover for Elliot would be the determining factor.

Where was Elliot?

I had this feeling he would flee. An undeniable feeling. I could feel him. I knew. I would wait to hear from Hawk first, though. I hit the shower in the meantime, phoning my client with the update. My head had a nice little grey bruise from the knock in the van. I crinkled my nose and looked away from the mirror. Tricky to talk to him, technically I couldn't announce Clope as the killer. I just let the client hear a snippet of the tape. It was a federal case now, so I couldn't release it to him, either. But he knew. I revealed it without saying anything. I hope it brought him closer to peace and resolution.

"I knew he had something to do with it! I knew it. You did what I asked. If he isn't caught, I want you to stay involved. I don't care what the feds say or do. You've done more for my son than they ever did. At least I know who now." His voice shuddered I thought he might break down on the phone. I truly felt for his loss and wished I could do more.

"I will, I promise. There's more to the story."

"Good. I want you to dig this guy into a grave. Slowly. Break him like he's broken me. Keep digging, Sara. I'm retired, and I want to see justice for Michael before I leave this earth. I want this guy exposed."

"I'll do my best." I mean, what more could I say? I didn't even know if I could deliver what he was asking. I did know Robert had a hold on me and I wanted to get to the bottom of the crimes. My client and I had that in common. Justice.

The conversation wrapped up quickly after that. This case had consumed me, day and night. It gave me a strange hangman feeling. It wasn't completely solved, and for my trouble I had a new adversary that could show up as anything. I wanted Hawk to call. I wanted to know what was going on. Maurice. That guy. I didn't have to wait to discover what happened to him. In the New York Daily News, fourth page, not the first.

Creative Director of Vogue, Maurice Grodman, quits.

I had no evidence on Maurice and thinking on it he wouldn't have called the cops. He would have said it was a robbery. Or turned it into something else. He was implicated. The Viper was still out there, and God knows what deal he made with that devil. This case had taken its toll. I would need a month to recoup – at least. I couldn't contact Evana, either, because if my line was tapped then the wrong people could hear. I had to wait it out. The phone rang ten hours later. I know because I counted.

"Tell me, Hawk. What happened?"

"He's gone."

"*WHAT?*" I knew exactly who he was talking about.

"What do you mean he's gone?" I cried out. I leapt up from the couch. "The deal didn't happen? He left? What? Where's Clope? What?"

"Take a breath, Sara. It's ok."

"It's not okay. This is crazy." Heart palpitations fluttered through my chest.

"He flew the coop. We got there too late. He hoodwinked us," Hawk told me in a disappointed voice.

"Hawk! You're the best in the business. How the fuck could he hoodwink you! You told me he was holding the drop at the warehouse!" I was screaming now I realized. I couldn't help it. This was insane.

"I missed the info on the stakeout. When my equipment went down for a minute and a half. I feel like that could have been crucial info. Remember he has a secret chamber? We were never going to catch it all."

"Clope's gone, too?" I probed as I raked my hands through my ebony locks.

"Yeah. They're working on a search warrant for his property, but the Elliots have strong legal teams in place. It's gridlock."

"U.S. Customs and Border Protection are being questioned." Hawk breathed out. "By the time they get the search warrant, any evidence will be gone, and it will all go away again. He may well be out of the country."

"How, Hawk?" I asked shaking my head in disillu-sionment.

"Many methods: car, plane, boat, airplane. I rule out cars, that's too risky. Pick one. We'll find out, but that's going to take a while," he said with a voice like still waters.

"The Elliots have gotten away with murder again," I lamented, as my stomach dropped. I wanted to drop the phone. Evana was right. This guy was untouchable. "I gotta go, Hawk. I can't deal with this."

"Sara. We are going to catch him. I've got a plan. I'm on the plane tonight to deliver the prototype. I've got someone covering the house. I'll text you the number and call Dermas if anything happens. Watch your back," he warned.

"What happened to Dean?" I asked quickly.

"He's home with his family. Under surveillance. So far so good," Hawk confirmed.

"Hawk, I gotta go. Call me when you land." I said with a heavy sigh. Elliot got away with it. How?

"Will do, over and out. Stay sane. Talk when I get back."

I got up from the couch in a stupor. I hadn't been out all day. This was horrendous. Elliot and now this twisted Viper guy were on the loose. Time to lie down. My mind was racing. A piece of paper caught my eye as I entered my bedroom for the first time. The corner of white popped up in my peripheral and made me cast my gaze to the ground. I got down on all fours to pick it up. The paper had blue hand-writing on it.

Nice try, Sara. You thought it was going to be that easy? Think again. We have unfinished business. I'll be in touch soon. Your move next.

Check Mate.

♟

ACKNOWLEDGMENTS

I want to give a shout out to the creative writing teacher who inspired me to write this story with a couple of photographs over four years ago. Thank you for opening my imagination to the dormant aspect of myself that craved awakening.

Shoutout to Sue Critz for her technical advice both in editing and in police tactics. Shoutout to the young graphic designer - Minaski who helped me with the cover.

Thank you to all of you. I want to acknowledge my readers also. Thank you for exploring the different worlds I'm taking you into! I'll keep them coming.

Yours in creativity,

L.R. STARR

ABOUT THE AUTHOR

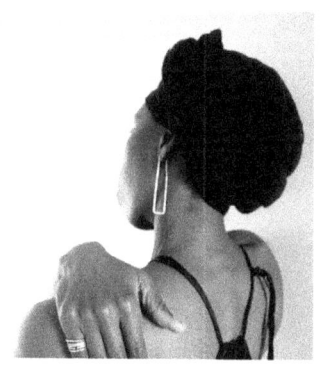

L.R. Starr is both a writer and professional artist residing in down under Australia. She is a lover of twists and turns and the uncovered mysteries of life. Never too far away from nature she can be found planning her next travels or in the realms of her imagination coming up with something creative to keep you inspired and entertained.

You can connect with the author here:
Facebook.com/L.R.STARR1
Twitter.com/AuthorIR
BookBub: www.bookbub.com/profile/l-r-starr

ALSO BY L. R. STARR

Check out the next book in the Sara Clemens Mystery Series while you're at it.

You can find the heat pounding page-turners below.

Firebomb

Pawn

Knight Time

If you enjoyed this series, it's highly likely that you would love the others in the Starr Mystery Series. There's more to come!

Murder on the Mountain

The Place That Sleeps

Bronte's Tale

Mob Ratbag